666

WOL-VRIEY

Other Books By Wol-vriey:

The Bizarro Story of I
Meat Suitcase
Chainsaw Cop Corpse
Vegan Zombie Apocalypse
Boston Posh (Bud Malone #1)
Vegan Vampire Vaginas
Vagina Mundi
Melanie Nemesis Catchpole
Bizarro 101: A Basic Primer
Boston Corpse (Bud Malone #2)
Dr. Orgasm
Boston Lust (Bud Malone #3)
Pussy Transmission
Hell Dancer
Girls Are Not Smiling
Brainchew
Brainchew 2: Out of Their Heads
Blue Nightmares
Daria (An Erotic Nightmare)
Wet Bones
Mr. Ugly
Brutal
Evil

Novellas and Short Stories By Wol-vriey

Big Trouble in Little Ass
Forever Ago Sunshine

666

WOL-VRIEY

Burning Bulb
PUBLISHING

666
By **Wol-vriey**

Burning Bulb Publishing
P.O. Box 4721
Bridgeport, WV 26330-4721
United States of America
www.BurningBulbPublishing.com

Cover designed by Gary Lee Vincent.
Author Photo: Lolade Akinsowon © 2014.

First Edition.

Paperback Edition ISBN: 978-1-948278-16-4

Printed in the United States of America

PROLOGUE

Al

The meeting took place outside of town, about a half-mile past the new church.

Al Gordon pulled his car—a red Ford Fiesta—up to the ruined shed that stood near the highway, got out and waited.

Overhead, the sky was a depressing shade of gray. All around him was dry sand and cacti. Fifty yards off was the oily Muskingum River; a mile beyond that the endless mountains.

Al Gordon was middle-aged. He had short black hair, unpleasant gray eyes, and quite large ears. He was dressed in neat denim overalls, a pale green shirt, and brown shoes.

Al sat on the hood of his car for a few minutes, collecting his courage about him. He stared up and down the highway, reassuring himself that he was doing the right thing. Looking towards town, he could just make out the church.

Finally, Al got up and entered the shed.

The shed contained no furniture. There was nothing in there except a trapdoor in the floor. After a last bout of worry, Al lifted the trapdoor and descended the revealed stone steps into the darkness below.

Once underground, Al clicked on a flashlight. He was in a stone-walled tunnel that stretched ahead maybe thirty feet to a dead end, before which lay the upper end of a downward stairway. Above him, the trapdoor yawned open, letting in what light it could.

Al set off along the tunnel.

He hoped the demoness would be waiting.

***

Al reached his destination after about twenty minutes of walking. The end of his quest was announced by a bright orange glow spilling from a door ahead. Al estimated that he was now about fifty feet below ground.

He flicked off his flashlight and entered the door, walking into a large stonewalled cavern. Two large smokeless fires burned at opposite ends of the stone hall. It was hot down here, but not unpleasantly so.

The demoness *was* waiting for him. She sat on one of several stone chairs arranged around the cavern.

She seemed a mingling of woman and cat. Though attractive, her head and face were feline in shape. She didn't have horns. She was naked—demons hardly ever wore clothes—and had furry red skin. Her hands and feet ended in long black claws. Her furry tail coiled from behind her and fell over her right thigh to dangle between her shapely legs, obscuring her sex from Al's view. Her leathery red wings were folded behind her.

Her face had the same jaded look of evil all demon faces did.

She smiled on seeing Al, revealing long fangs.

"Welcome," she said. "My name is Hexis. Who are you?"

"Al Gordon."

She seemed to taste his name on her tongue. "So . . . what do you want from me, Al?"

He told her.

She frowned, the look in her cat-eyes turning cold. "That's impossible. Surely you know that. Such things are not permitted here, even for us devils."

Al spat on the floor. "Don't give me that crap, lady. Everything's possible if you're desperate enough."

Hexis regarded him with new interest. "Yes, you're right. But are *you* desperate enough, Al Gordon?"

It took him a few moments to get the words out. Then he nodded. "Yeah, I fucking am desperate enough."

She laughed. "Alright then. Give me a minute to check this out below."

Al nodded again. Hexis vanished from her chair.

Al spent the interim of her disappearance pacing the stone cavern. He walked near to one of the fires that lit the space, enduring the heat of its blaze for a closer look. The fire burnt to about human height.

As he'd expected, there was neither coal nor firewood on the ground there. The flames emerged from a jagged crack in the floor.

Al realized he'd not been the first person to come down here, possibly to strike a similar deal. To the rear of the fire, lying against the wall, was a corpse—roasted black, with its skull cracked open by the relentless heat.

Gulping, Al quickly backed away. When he turned around, he found Hexis waiting for him. He was startled, he'd not heard her return. But then, she'd made no noise on vanishing either.

Now the demoness was standing and was holding a large book bound in human skin. Even three feet away from it, Al sensed the book's power and malevolence.

"Volume 666 of the LOTUS, just as you requested," Hexis informed him drolly.

He noted the amusement in her voice. Did she plan on tricking him? She was a demoness, after all, and he knew demons couldn't be trusted.

She held the book out to him.

He reached out a hand to take it from her. She waited till his fingers were just touching the skin-covered volume, then jerked it away.

"Not so fast, human," she said with a cold smile that chilled him to the marrow. "You know there's payment involved."

He frowned. "Stop toying with me, woman. Just tell me what you want and I'll do it."

She walked around him, her bare breasts pressing against his back as she did so, her tail tickling his thighs. She leaned her slim body on his right shoulder and blew in his ear, then whispered, "This is a contract. You can't back out of it. It's for real, baby."

"Yes, yes! I understand," he growled impatiently. "Just tell me what the conditions are, and I'll—YEOW!"

A blazing pain had suddenly flared up on the right side of Al's head. He flung up his hand to investigate and pulled it away soaked with red. It took him a few seconds to realize that the demoness had bitten his ear completely off.

He spun around and gaped at her. She was laughing while chewing the severed ear, with blood running over her lips and down her chin.

On a reflex, Al slapped her. The blow shifted her slightly, but it had felt like hitting a wall.

"My ear—you stupid bitch! You . . . you . . . shit!"

She moved incredibly fast then. One moment she was right in front of Al, and the next moment he couldn't see her anymore. But he felt her alright. This time, to torment him, she did it a little slower. Al felt her hands grip his head and shoulders and before he could push her away, felt her kiss his left ear, then slip her lips over it as if to suck on it. Then, the next moment, he felt the same indescribable pain again as her teeth once more came together in his flesh.

He screamed, and when she let go of him, clamped both hands to the sides of his head to stop the bleeding. Behind him, he could hear her laughing.

When he could focus through his pain, Al turned to gaze at Hexis. The red demoness grinned coyly back at him. She'd returned to sit in her chair. While chewing his left ear—Al could see the flesh shredding in her mouth—she was stroking her sex as if sexually aroused.

Al felt like killing her.

"You crazy bitch!" he growled at her. "You've eaten both of my goddamn ears!" He was finding it hard to hear: the blood was trickling into his ear canals.

The demoness shrugged and swallowed. "Merely sealing the deal. Would you have preferred it if I'd told you first that part of the payment for the book would be your ears?"

Al was about to reply with an angry "Yes!" when he cottoned on to what she'd said. Worry instantly replaced his rage.

"*Part* payment?" he growled instead. "You're gonna take something else from me?"

Hexis parted her thighs wider, rubbed her vagina vigorously, and shook her head. She licked the remainder of his blood off her lips, then gasped: "Not unless . . not unless you offer the flesh freely to me."

Her voice now sounded weirdly filtered to Al, who'd finally removed his hands from his head. The blood still dribbled from his wounds, but the heat in the cavern seemed to be helping it clot. "You're insane if you think I'd ever voluntarily give you a part of my body to eat. That ain't *ever* gonna happen. Hell no! There's no chance in Hell of that happening."

Still caressing her sex, she smiled through her erotic pleasure. "No chance in *Hell*, Al?"

"You know what the hell I mean!"

The demoness gasped and had an orgasm. Wincing with pain, Al sat on the edge of a stone chair and waited for her to finish climaxing and resume their conversation. His clothes were covered with his blood. The twin fires filled the cavern with horrible brooding shadows.

Once Hexis's orgasmic trembling had subsided, she gestured to the chair beside Al's, on which the skin-bound tome lay. "Listen, Al, the book is now yours. But . . ." She had a sexually-sated laxity to her now that was interfering with her speech. "But . . . you'll be required to render us a service now and again."

"What sort of a service?"

"A bloody service. One that will involve killing. Murder."

Al didn't immediately reply. Murder? This was anything but what he'd planned for. This was totally unforeseen.

Doing his best to ignore the burning pain of his missing ears, he wiped his hands clean on an unbloodied portion of his overalls, then picked the book up. He immediately felt its evil aura welcoming him, just as he noticed that, like a sponge, the book had instantly soaked up all the blood that remained on his hands.

Well, he'd gotten what he'd come for. But at what a nasty price. And there was more to pay?

He forced the words through his agony. "I can't murder . . . I just wanna—"

She silenced him with a gesture. She spoke coldly, harshly: "You have no choice, Al Gordon. Without murder, without a whole lot of violent bloodshed, that which you want"—she gestured at the book he held—"will be eternally inaccessible to you."

He sighed, blood dribbling down both sides of his head. "Okay, okay, I'll do your dirty work for you. Just call me when you need me. But I gotta warn you, lady, I've never killed anyone before. I might screw it up."

The red demoness got to her feet. Sexual moisture dribbling down her shapely thighs, she approached Al. She laughed. "Oh, we've got just the right victim for you to practice on."

Al Gordon listened to Hexis explain what she and the other demons wanted done, and after a while he began laughing too.

Yeah, killing that sonofabitch would be good payback for losing his ears.

CHAPTER 1

Duncan & Edie

Heading north for Dresden, the sleek silver Nissan Altima rolled smoothly along Ohio's State Route 666. It was about 6 p.m. in the evening, on a pleasant Saturday in late spring.

The vehicle's driver was a handsome thirtyish man named Duncan White; tall and with brown hair and eyes. His passenger was a pretty young woman named Edith (or 'Edie') Forrest, a blue-eyed blonde. Both were dressed casually though expensively, as fitted wealthy lovers out for a fun weekend.

Duncan White handled the silver car with ease and confidence. His expression was grim though. Occasionally, he'd glance sideways at his lovely passenger. She in turn would giggle back at him, then reach over and stroke his arm, which invariably made him flinch.

There was an unspoken tension in the car that Duncan couldn't avoid and Edie seemed not to notice. Or if she did notice, she acted like she didn't.

"How much further, baby?" she asked Duncan, once again placing her hand on his arm. This time she didn't remove her fingers when he flinched, but instead tightened her grip on his muscles, playfully squeezed, and dug her fingers into them. "Man, I'm soooo tired. Once we reach the motel, I'm gonna fall asleep immediately. Just wake me up when you need some ass. So, how much further to Dresden?"

He glanced at her hand, then at her face. "Not much further." He forced a smile. "Edie, are you sure you didn't tell anyone you were seeing me? If word of this somehow gets back to Cheryl, I'll be screwed—finished."

She pouted, dropping her hand from his arm to his thigh and squeezing. "Relax, baby. I'm not some dizzy teenager with a crush. I know what I'm doing."

He grimaced. "I dare say you do."

They'd met up in Zanesville thirty minutes ago, arriving there separately though they both lived and worked in Columbus. On his suggestion neither of them had told their circle of friends and family where they were off to.

Duncan had made certain that his girlfriend Cheryl Dawson hadn't the slightest inkling that he was off to spend the weekend with her good friend Edie.

Edie laughed. "It'll be just fine, you'll see. We'll have lots of fucking fun . . . and lots of fun fucking."

"I need to stop for gas," Duncan announced as they reached a filling station named the Red Eagle, a self-service place with a convenience store.

Duncan pulled smoothly into the Red Eagle gas station.

Once he'd parked by a pump, Edie got out of the car. "I wanna get some stuff in the shop," she said.

"Alright. Don't take too long."

"I won't. Do you want anything?"

"Nope, maybe later, when we go out for dinner."

He watched her hurry off, her slim body limber and pleasing in her sleeveless red dress, her feet clicking audibly on the concrete floor, her blonde hair hanging halfway down her back.

"She's just lovely—it's such a pity that I'm gonna have to kill her," he said to himself. "Regrettable as hell, but she's gotta go."

Duncan White felt real regret over what he was going to do to Edie Forrest this weekend, but he also saw no other possible solution to the dilemma she presented him with. The dread anticipation of actually committing a murder seemed about to pulp his mind. It was that intense.

I just need to maintain a semblance of normalcy, give her what she wants . . . and then . . .

Unaware of the danger she was in, Edie vanished through the door of the convenience store. Duncan shrugged and focused on buying gas.

While filling his tank, he looked around. His car was currently the only one at the gas station. The station was a medium-sized place and well-maintained too, amidst its forest backdrop. But Duncan felt something out of place about it. In some mysterious way, the Red Eagle 'felt' older than it looked.

He felt a chill go through him as he regarded the place, but he put the feeling down to cold feet concerning his intended act of murder.

A plastic bag in hand, Edie was walking back towards him. Duncan sighed. He didn't really *want* to kill her, but . . . but . . . the whole situation was impossible.

"Hey, you okay?" she asked on reaching the car. Then, before he could respond, she added, "There's something weird about this place, you know."

"How do you mean?" he asked. "Did the shop attendant act weird to you?"

She shook her head, a frown on her pretty face. "Not like that. It's just a feeling I have—like, maybe I should have stayed at home today."

Duncan nodded. "Yeah, I sense it too. For some reason, this place gives me the creeps."

She dropped her shopping bag on the front seat then stared at him over the car's roof. "And it ain't just here, man. Ever since we began motoring along this damn 666 road with all these ghostlike trees . . . the atmosphere has been all wrong, like . . ." Words failed her and she gestured helplessly around.

Out on the highway, a brown Lexus SUV heading the other way, towards Zanesville, was paused on the shoulder waiting for a Dresden-bound truck to roll past so that the SUV could cross the road into the Red Eagle. Beyond the SUV and just visible between the trees that lined the road, the Muskingum River stretched parallel to Route 666, flowing sluggishly like a liquefied highway.

Duncan looked uneasy. "Let's hit the road again."

"Yeah, the sooner we're off this creepy highway, the better."

"Try not to worry and I won't either."

She winked at him. "I love a dude with a positive attitude . . . Oh, shit, baby. Tired as I am, I'm impatient to get you into bed and have myself a bit of what Cheryl takes for granted. That hand job I gave you was just to warm you up."

Duncan winced at the memory. They both worked for the Cashstretch retail chain. Yesterday lunchtime, she'd insisted on masturbating him in the office. "See, I know exactly what you like," she'd said as he ejaculated through the tight circle of her fingers.

Shivering nervously, Edie got into the car.

Duncan remained standing by the vehicle. Over on his right, the brown SUV had crossed the highway and was just pulling into the gas station. The vehicle's passengers all seemed to be young men.

He forgot the SUV, returned his thoughts to his companion. *Oh yes, I am going to kill this bitch . . . I'm gonna to stab her to death and rip her guts out and there's nothing on this damn planet that'll stop me doing so!*

"Baby, I'm waiting," Edie called. "Please, get in the car and let's leave this place!"

Duncan calmed down and got into the car.

***

It happened right as they drove out of the gas station. Duncan couldn't say *what* exactly had occurred, but something definitely had. For a moment he'd felt a gentle resistance against his chest, as if he was pushing through a flimsy barrier. He'd had a sense of the barrier 'crackling' and next thing, it was over.

"Hey, did you feel that?" Edie asked nervously. "It was like electricity just sparked all over my body. It seemed to pass through the entire car too."

Duncan looked ahead and froze. Then he looked in the rearview mirror. Then he parked the car.

"Why'd you stop?" Edie asked. She was looking at him and hadn't noticed anything amiss yet. "I'm fine, it was just a weird feeling, that's all. I'm not sick or anything."

"Look back, out of the rear window," Duncan said.

"Why?"

"Just look out of the rear window, Edie." His voice was taut, as if he was barely holding himself back from screaming.

Frowning, Edie did so. She swiveled her body on her seat and stared out of the rear window. Then, confused, she looked back at him. "Duncan, where did the gas station vanish to? And the forest too?"

Duncan didn't reply. He just sat staring out of the windshield at the road ahead—Route 666—which now ran through a landscape which clearly wasn't the one they'd earlier been traveling on.

After a while, Edie asked the question on his mind: "Duncan, where the hell are we now?"

CHAPTER 2

Rick, Randy, Manny & Cody

"I wonder why they don't just rename this fucker," Rick Price said as he pulled up at the first fuel pump.

"How d'you mean, bro?" his younger brother Randy asked from the backseat of the Lexus SUV. Randy was sitting behind Rick.

Rick shrugged as he cut the engine. "You know, like they did the other one down in . . ." He gazed left at the young man in the front passenger seat. "Dude, you're the think-tank. Which state was it again?"

Manny Bishop thought a bit. "*States* actually . . . US Route 666 served the 'Four Corners' area down south—Colorado, Utah, Arizona and New Mexico."

"So what happened to it?" Randy asked, looking as he did so at Cody Clark, the vehicle's fourth passenger, who was half-asleep beside him on the backseat.

"Everyone called it the Devil's Highway, so the authorities changed the route's number 'cos no one wanted to drive on it," Manny informed Randy, then looked at Rick. "The route also ran through Navajo Indian territory, and *they* were pissed off 'cos the government wasn't repairing the road either. They finally changed it to . . . what was it now? I think . . . 491?"

"I remember reading about that one," Randy said. "Ha ha ha! They changed the route number and everyone stole the '666' signs. One guy even reputedly crashed his car into a signpost to break its welding."

"Yeah," Rick agreed. "That was just crazy, man. I recall even seeing some of them for sale on eBay."

Rick got out to buy the gas. He was a slim young man, pale-eyed and with his head shaven. Dressed in tee shirt and denim like his friends. Stereotypes aside, Rick Price looked exactly what he was—a young auto mechanic. His younger brother Randy was still in college. Manny and Cody both worked for InterMind, an IT company.

All four were in their mid-twenties, with Randy being three years younger than Rick.

Rick stood there in the cool evening. A wayward breeze tickled his bare scalp. The gas station clock said the time was a minute past 6 p.m.

For a moment he felt extra weird. *Where the hell did that silver Nissan go to?* Rick was certain the Nissan had been driving out of the gas station when they'd driven in, but now it was nowhere in sight. To crosscheck, he looked up and down the highway. No, the silver car was gone.

No one else seemed to have noticed anything amiss. Manny and Randy were arguing about the size of Jennifer Lawrence's breasts. Cody looked more alert now, but dopey, with a 'slightly stoned' smile on his face and his sandy hair tousled up.

Everyone except Rick, who'd been doing all their driving today, had had a few beers.

Feeling creeped out, Rick got out his credit card and punched his gas purchase info into the pump. He couldn't get over the way the silver car had seemed to vanish into thin air.

***

The Price brothers and their two friends were returning from a fishing trip up near Conesville. The four had been friends since high school and now all lived and worked in or around Zanesville.

The fishing trip had been Manny's idea. He'd been telling the others for months—really bugging them—about this great sheltered angling cove he knew up north. So they'd finally picked this Saturday to make the trip.

It had been a great trip. They'd had fun, met a few young local women and gotten their phone numbers, and caught lots of fish—mostly bass and walleye. Two cooler-loads of fish now sat in the trunk, along with their fishing rods and tackle and a small mountain of empty beer bottles.

They'd considered staying overnight in Conesville and doing some more fishing on Sunday, but Manny had insisted that he had to get back to Zanesville tonight to handle a sudden emergency for his mother.

And here they were now, hurrying home to mommy.

Rick smirked as he held the fuel nozzle in the tank and waited for it to fill up. Manny Bishop sometimes acted oddball like that. Their stopping here now—their running out of gas in the first place—was Manny's fault too. Rick had wanted to fill up in Conesville but Manny had said he knew this place along the highway . . .

(They all cut Manny some slack, because he still hadn't gotten over his girlfriend's abduction two years ago. He and Michelle Walz had just begun dating and then a serial killer had snatched Michelle.)

Manny got out of the car. "Need to use the restroom," he told Rick.

"Don't take your time," Rick called after him as he loped off towards the convenience store, scratching his blonde hair. "You're the one who's in such a damn hurry to get home."

"Won't be a minute."

Manny was back in two minutes. Rick was already back in the driver's seat waiting. Behind him, his brother was humming a Slain Jane tune, to which Cody was making drum sounds with his mouth.

"Alright, let's roll," Manny said, checking his watch as he settled into his seat. "Shit, I hope I'm not late."

"Stop worrying, mommy's boy. I'll get you home to mama on time."

Rick put the SUV in motion and steered it out of the gas station.

Just like before, there was a truck coming that he had to wait for before he could cross to the other lane. (Afterwards, Rick did wonder if maybe avoiding that delay would have prevented what happened. But by then it was too late.)

The truck passed. As Rick eased his car out of the gas station, they all felt it at the same time.

"What the hell just happened!?" Cody yelped. "I felt like the car just shocked me."

"Me too," Randy agreed from beside Cody. "Yeah, like I just pushed through an electric wall. Or it went through me."

"Guys, where have all the trees vanished to?" Manny asked in a worried voice. "They're all gone."

"The fuck just happened?" Rick asked, posing the question more to himself than to the others. "What the fuck just happened?"

He looked up and down the highway. They'd just gotten onto the road when he'd felt that electric strangeness roll over him. The truck that had just passed them had been shrinking in the distance, and a bright red car had been approaching from the opposite direction. And now . . .

Just like with the silver Nissan earlier, both the truck and red car had abruptly vanished. Left and right of Rick's SUV, the road was free of any traffic. And like Manny had said, all the trees were gone too.

"You're not gonna like this news," Cody said, "but the gas station has vanished too."

After confirming that to be true, Rick just managed to drive across the highway. Then he parked the car and they all got out.

***

The four young men stood by the brown SUV, staring around them in confusion, slowly taking in the relentless shocks of this strange place they'd somehow found themselves in.

"The sun is black," Manny said.

"At one end of the highway the sky is vagina-pink and at the other it's Goth-black."

"Where'd all the trees and grass vanish to? It's just rocks and cacti everywhere. Are those mountains over there?"

"Shit, bro, yeah."

"Where the hell are we? That's what *I* wanna know?"

CHAPTER 3

Duncan & Edie

"Well, at least the Muskingum River's still here," Edie said. "Though now it looks like it's flowing with crude oil."

Duncan looked sharply at her. They'd walked across the highway to look at the river. She was right: the river channel did seem full of oil-spill; and there were no trees growing on its banks anymore. No grass either—just sand and hot rocks. Worse still, the river stank like rotting fish and rotten eggs.

The evening weather had now turned warm.

The worst detail of all, however, the one that made Duncan White go pale with fear, was something Edie hadn't mentioned: the mountains. On each side of the road/river, about a mile distant either way, two mountain ranges ran parallel to each other. These immense unbroken walls of rock extended as far as Duncan's eyes could make out. In one direction the mountain ranges merged into a dark and forbidding haze that blended with the gray sky overhead, while in the opposite direction they blended into pretty pink mist.

The countryside between the towering walls was all bare rock and sand, with lots of evil-looking cacti. There may have been houses in the distance, but they were too far away to tell.

And overhead . . . that black evil-looking circle?

The sun is black. My God, how can the sun be black?

Duncan didn't know what was going on, but it was clearly Edie's fault. She was determined to mess things up for him. Looked like she'd succeeded big-time.

However, he didn't say a word to Edie. He feared that if he did, and she gave him some cool, smart-aleck reply, he'd be unable to resist the urge to get the razor-sharp hunting knife out of the car and start butchering her right here. And though, yes, Duncan did plan on killing

14

Edie very soon, he wasn't about doing it out in the open where the cops might nab him. No, he'd do it just the way he'd planned it—in a motel room in . . .

In . . . where? Where the hell is this place? Where are we?

So instead, Duncan merely nodded meekly and turned and headed for his car again. After a short interval, he heard Edie's quick footsteps as she hurried after him. She took his arm. He didn't even bother to shake her off.

"I was right, baby," Edie said miserably. "I really should have stayed home." She shivered. "From the look of this sky though, I'd say it might take us quite a while to get back home again."

CHAPTER 4

Rick, Randy, Manny & Cody

Rick drove the car towards the 'dark zone' of the sky. It was either that way or the other. Also, the dark zone was the direction in which the SUV had been pointed after they'd crossed the road. That direction was where Zanesville ought to be. Hopefully, this whole thing was merely a shared hallucination they were all experiencing.

Towards either end of the route, the air appeared hazy.

About a mile inland on either side of the road rose steep gray canyon-like walls. As far as any of them could tell, these opposing rock faces ran parallel to each other without any break in their continuity, and both seemed to touch the sky above, leaving between their tops the two-mile-wide stretch of gray firmament in which the black sun favored the world with its sickly fluorescent glare.

"It's like we're trapped in a crazy stone tunnel with the sky as the roof," Cody said. The sandy-haired boy was fully awake now, his eyes seemingly propped open by his disbelief.

"Don't worry about it, man," Randy said, the look on his face exactly like Cody's.

Indeed, all four of the young men had the same look of awe and fear.

Manny seemed slightly less perturbed than the others. "I'm sure if we keep driving we'll find a way out," he said.

"Yeah," Rick agreed in an unconvinced tone of voice. "There's gotta be a way outa here somewhere. Maybe one of these turnoffs."

They were just passing another turnoff. They'd already passed several, all leading, as far as they could see, to dead ends at the mountain range. Those on their right had bridges across the river. So far the turnoffs didn't look like exits.

"Guys," Cody said nervously, "the gas station *vanished*. Like it walked off and left us behind. Stuff like that doesn't happen in real life. And also, you saw the damn river—I don't think that stuff in it was water, and—"

"Calm down," Rick quickly interrupted him. "Dude, just frigging calm down. Like Manny says, we'll find a way outa here."

"What if we can't?" Cody's voice had risen in pitch; its nervousness reflecting his companions' worries. "This damn place doesn't even seem to be on Earth—we seem to have driven into some goddamn sci-fi movie. Look at everywhere—dry desert, brown sand as far as those damn cliff sides. None of our cellphones work anymore . . . and . . . and . . . and, guys, we haven't seen a single car on the highway since we found ourselves here. What if we can't get back home again?"

Rick gripped the steering wheel tight as he stared down the barren highway ahead, the view in the rearview mirror just as barren. The road wasn't straight, it bend to and fro like a snake slithering through the desert. His jaw and neck muscles tightened with anger. His intended retort was however cut off by his younger brother Randy, who joked: "Well, in that case, considering the state of the river, we're lucky we already got all our fishing done, ain't we?"

"We gotta still be on Earth," Manny contended. "Though I gotta agree, this place gives me the damn creeps too. It's like we somehow fell into the bottom of the Grand Canyon."

"With a *black* sun overhead? Or haven't you noticed that yet?"

"Cody, for chrissakes, give it a rest!" Rick growled.

Grumbling something about "God-damned Devil's highway Route 666," that the others all pretended not to hear, Cody settled back in his seat and kept quiet. After a while he began nervously worrying his sandy hair.

"Well, there's houses here," Manny said two minutes later. "Thank heavens."

The two guys in the backseat leaned out of their windows for a look. About two miles ahead they saw signs of civilization.

"Yeah," Rick agreed cautiously as they neared the distant buildings. "See, Cody, man? Nothing to worry about. Houses mean people. Folks live here."

"Yeah," Randy agreed. "We'll be able to ask directions home."

***

They rolled down the highway, passing more dead-end turnoffs. The houses grew nearer.

Their destination seemed to be the outskirts of a town. But as the town got closer, so too did the once-distant wall of blackness at the road's end.

This latter observation bothered Manny. From miles off, the darkness had seemed liquid and swirling; now it appeared to be a solid thing, like a painted wall. And now also, the darkness seemed to be bleeding into the air. Here the light from the black sun was dimmer. They appeared to be travelling from afternoon into late evening, into a sunset zone as it were.

Manny had also noticed that up ahead, the unbroken mountain ranges on either side of the highway and corrupted river appeared to converge towards the darkness, as if they both became the darkness, and this place—wherever this was—abruptly ended there.

This suspicion/discovery wasn't something Manny was about pointing out to the others, of course. Not with the way Cody seemed close to freaking out. And Rick seemed about to lose it too.

"Shit, look at this place!" Rick said as the SUV rolled past the first houses. "Is this a dump or what?"

"I don't like this, bro," Randy said. "These are all ruins, old frigging ruins."

Cody said nothing. He just looked scared.

The first buildings *were* ruins. And they looked weird too. Some looked like Southern antebellum houses, others looked like medieval European buildings. A few were Frontier-style log cabins. What they all shared was their antiquity and run-down state.

At first the buildings just dotted the highway, but they thickened in number the farther along Rick drove. There was no one outside the houses; not even outside the less damaged ones.

Up ahead, where the concentration of old buildings formed a town, Manny thought he saw large birds filling the darkened sky. Seeing the birds filled him with apprehension. Suddenly, Manny didn't feel like visiting the approaching town.

He turned to Rick, but to his relief, Rick was already slowing the SUV.

"What you stopping for, bro?" Randy asked from the backseat.

Rick turned to face him. "I don't like the way the sky looks up ahead. It's like a damn thunderstorm over there. I'm thinking we should knock on a few doors first."

"These are all ruins," Cody pointed out.

"Yeah, they are," Rick readily agreed, "but some of 'em are less ruined than others. Take this one, for instance"—he gestured out of the car at an ancient building set about twenty yards in from the highway. "It looks habitable enough."

"Yeah, but we haven't seen anyone since getting here."

Rick pointed an angry finger at Cody. "Man, we're gonna knock on that damn front door and that's frigging that."

Manny had been studying the old house. Built partly from dark stone, the squat ugly building sat at the end of a paved walkway. It had a deep shadowy porch, large windows, and a white door. Its most impressive characteristic (other than the fact that it was in better condition than its neighbors) were the two gargoyles perched at either end of the roof. Manny found the gargoyles' location odd; to his quite analytical mind, this building lacked the gothic character to require such decorations.

The decorative stone beasts looked like others of their ilk: apelike bodies with bat wings folded behind them, long claws on hands and feet, and grotesque faces. These faces were almost all mouth—jaws that were deep slashes in their noseless oblong heads, with lips curled back over long teeth that locked together. The creatures were jet black in color and even from a distance looked distressingly realistic. Were it not that they'd not moved once while he'd been staring at them, Manny would have assumed they were living creatures.

As it was, his consideration of the gargoyles was cut short by Cody saying, "Look, man—there's no one on the fucking highway. Let's keep rolling until we do find someone."

"No," Rick insisted.

"I really don't feel like getting out of the car, bro," Randy admitted. "This damn place is so spooky."

"He's got a point," Manny said, rejoining the conversation. "Even the silver car that was pulling out of the filling station when we drove in isn't here."

Rick nodded, his eyes bothered. "I've been thinking that myself. They should be here too."

"Maybe everyone's over the other way?" Cody suggested. "Back down at the pink end of this blasted road?"

"Guys, look," Randy said, opening his door, "let's just do like my bro says. It won't take us more than five minutes. Besides, this house is the only one in good condition as far as I can see. If there's anyone living around here, this is the most likely place they'll be."

"Except they're ghouls," Cody said. "But, alright." He opened the offside rear door and stepped down. Then he stood staring over at the mountain ranges that hemmed them in on both sides. It was impossible how high those stone walls rose; almost like they went up forever, the walls of a giant room, with the negative sun dangling like a light bulb between their upper reaches. He shivered though the air was warm.

"You coming or not?" Rick called.

"Yeah, sure." Cody headed up the walk after the others.

CHAPTER 5

Teeth & Tentacles

The four friends were halfway up the walk when the unexpected happened.

Manny had been looking down the highway, studying the strange birds that filled the sky over the town. But the light was too dim there to see them clearly.

At a noise behind him, Manny spun around and gaped.

The two gargoyles on the building's roof—both previously motionless statues—were now flying down toward them. The creatures swept down with clear attacking intent, their jaws and claws spread wide, monstrous black wings flapping above them. Both were the size of chimpanzees. In the glance Manny had of them before ducking out of their way, he saw that their eyes were yellow and snakelike and glittered with both evil and hunger.

Rick, Manny, and Randy all ducked. The gargoyles flew over them and hit Cody, who, still unconvinced of the wisdom of their stopping here, was lagging ten feet behind the others.

The gargoyles sank their claws into Cody's chest, belly and back. Next, while he gushed blood and screamed in agony, they lifted him into the air and, hovering there in midair, tore him to pieces.

Manny almost pissed himself as above them, Cody Clark exploded into a bloody mess and his freed guts fell out of him. After a final scream of terror, Cody gave up the ghost. Then one of the gargoyles took Cody's entire face into its mouth. With a bowel-loosening noise, the monster cracked open Cody's skull and swallowed its front half, face and all. The other gargoyle was clawing its way into Cody's chest and pulling out the pinkish mass of his lungs and stuffing them in its mouth. Beneath the feeding creatures, Cody's dangling guts swung violently to and fro like red bells ringing.

Already by the porch steps, Rick, Manny and Randy ran up them and across the shadowy porch to the front door. Rick began banging. "Help! Someone, let us in! Open this damn door!"

"There's no one in there!" Randy said, his eyes wide with fright. While his older brother kept pounding and demanding to be let into what he suspected was an empty house, Randy walked along the front wall and began trying the windows.

Manny was standing in the porch doorway; looking up at where, barely ten yards away and fifteen feet up in the air, the pair of nightmare creatures were still busily gobbling down one of their friends. The gargoyles made a racket as they fought over the choice parts of the human corpse, squawking like enraged birds and clawing at each other in their bloodlust, with the beating of their dark wings an additional thunder. The creatures were by now drenched in Cody's blood, the rest of which was splattered far and wide across the front walkway.

Rick ceased banging on the door and stepped up besides Manny. "Dude," he said, "we'd better run back for the ride while those damn things are still occupied with Cody. Or else we're gonna be next."

Manny looked sharply at him. Rick's face was tight with tension. He noticed how Rick was clearly making an effort to look away from the monsters that were eating Cody right next to them.

"Quick! Back into the car!" Rick yelled. "Go!"

"Hey, guys, wait!" Randy called from behind them. "I've gotten a window open—NOOOOOOOO!"

They spun around and gaped. Something had a hold of Randy. They couldn't make out what it actually was—it looked as though the shadows at the far end of the porch had reached out tentacles and wrapped Randy in them. Randy was enfolded in those flailing coils of darkness and was being pulled back into their source, with more black tentacles flinging themselves around him each moment.

In just a few seconds, all they could see of Randy were his blinking right eye and his left hand, which clutched desperately at the air. Like a body lying in a bed and covered with a black sheet, the rest of him was all wrapped up in those living shadows. To Manny's eyes, the thing that had Randy seemed to be part of the wall; maybe the house itself, transformed at that point.

"Hold on, bro!" Rick yelled. "I'm coming."

He took two steps forward, then froze. Randy had begun screaming, and below him, a pool of blood was spreading across the porch floor. Then there came a loud noise from inside the darkness, as if someone had just pulverized something with a sledgehammer. Simultaneously, Randy quit screaming. Next moment, the dark coils parted in the middle and spat out something.

Rick stared. The thing the darkness had ejected was a fleshless human skeleton.

Rick stood there frozen. "Little bro . . . !"

Then Manny grabbed him and ran him down off the front porch and towards the SUV.

Above them, the gargoyles were noisily disputing possession of Cody's legs. Rick and Manny ignored them and raced for their car.

Then they stopped. Like a strike of negative lightning, a black streak suddenly hit the SUV, its impact totally crumpling the SUV's roof. A moment later, the black missile—another gargoyle—righted itself and after giving them a cold stare, began shredding the vehicle's roof, its claws ripping the metal apart with ease. While Rick and Manny watched in horror, two more gargoyles flew down at the SUV and joined the first one in shredding it. One of them quickly punctured both of the vehicle's offside tires. The tires didn't just hiss out—they exploded, dumping the rims directly on the ground.

"We're fucked," Manny said. "They're destroying the ride so we can't get away. Once they're done with it, we're next."

Indeed, the gargoyle that had been savaging the SUV's roof was now perched on its hood. The horrible creature seemed to be trying to decide which of them to attack first.

Another of the gargoyles had torn open the vehicle's trunk, opened up the fish-filled coolers in there and was eating up their catch of bass and walleye, scattering the remnants everywhere.

"We'd better run back to the house," Rick said coldly. "Try to break down the door."

Then there was a loud screeching of tires to their left, a gunshot, and the head of the gargoyle that had been staring at them exploded in a mess of blood. The creature toppled through the SUV's front windscreen, which was now devoid of glass. Another gunshot noise and a second gargoyle's head was blown off. This one fell onto the curb and lay there with blood gushing from its neck stump, its black wings flapping as though it were flying.

"Over here, you two! Quick!"

They ran over to the black pickup truck that had just pulled up ten yards away. The GMC truck was heavily reinforced with metal plating; it looked almost like a small tank. The truck driver was standing by its door with a shotgun to his shoulder, and was already firing again, this time up above them.

From the following nonhuman shriek of pain, both young men deduced that he'd just blown a pursuing gargoyle out of the air.

Then they piled into the front of the pickup truck; Manny in the middle, Rick by the door.

After a final shot that missed its target, the driver got in beside them. He was in his mid-forties, blonde, and had a mustache and long beard; he was dressed in denim, boots, and a Baltimore Orioles baseball cap. He dropped his smoking shotgun on the truck's backseat, started up the engine, and pulled a quick U-turn. A moment later, they were speeding in the opposite direction.

"Sorry I was late," their rescuer said in a southern drawl after a sideways glance at them. "I almost forgot that tonight was the sixth of June."

Neither Manny nor Rick said anything. Manny because he was still struck speechless; Rick because he was trying not to shed tears over his brother's passing.

"You guys went the wrong way," the blonde driver said. "Happens a lot to newbies; then the 'goyles eat 'em before I can reach 'em. Either that or the damn shadow-things get 'em."

"Thanks for rescuing us back there, man," Rick said.

"Yeah, thanks," Manny added. "Hey, who are you? And where the hell are we?"

"Yeah. What is this place?"

The man laughed grimly. "Hello to you both," he replied. "My name's Ned Shriver. Welcome to Hell, boys."

CHAPTER 6

Ned, Manny & Rick

"Hell?" Manny asked.

Ned took his eyes off the road long enough to nod at him. "Yeah, Hell. But not like you know it from the Good Book. This place is like a demonic outpost, ya see." Ned gestured out of the window at the passing landscape. "Just look at it—except for the mountains walling us in, it's like the goddamn Wild West frontier."

Manny gulped and nodded. As if giving them a sightseeing tour, Ned had slowed his pickup truck once they'd left the old gothic houses behind. They weren't exactly crawling along, but they could have been moving a lot faster.

"Why are you driving so slow?" Manny asked. "More danger up ahead?"

Ned shook his head. "Nah, I always do this with new arrivals, give them time to get acclimatized to things before dropping them off in town. You got any questions, now's the time to ask 'em, 'cos I generally don't hang around town."

They could see the town right ahead, about three miles distant. Nearer to them, a number of widely spaced houses dotted the roadside.

They were just about reaching one of these, a little stone shed on their right and about fifty yards in from the highway, when Ned pulled up to the side of the road.

Ned parked the pickup truck, then swiveled in his seat to face the two perplexed and scared young men. "But first, before you start with the questions, lemme give you my standard introductory lecture about this place. There's some important info you guys need to have to survive down here."

Rick, who'd been sitting moodily since their escape from the gargoyles, now broke his silence: "Man, what the hell were those flying things back there?" he asked in a choked voice, blinking back tears from his eyes. "And what was that black thing that killed my brother?"

"Just call the flying things what they look like: gargoyles or 'goyles for short. They're hell creatures, demon beasts."

"Demons? You killed three of them."

"Didn't kill 'em; just damaged 'em a li'l. Something always repairs the winged shits."

"And the other thing? The one that got Randy?"

"Describe it."

Rick was overcome with emotion, so Manny gave the description for him: "It was black, man, like the shadows on the wall of the building suddenly came alive and plucked Randy up in their tentacles. Then, after sucking him into itself, it opened up again and spat out his bones."

Rick let out a loud sob.

Ned shook his head. "That was one of the damn shadow-things. They're everywhere around here and are one of the dangers I was gonna warn ya about." He gestured at the barren landscape, the rock walls, the endless sand. "You gotta be very careful down here; lotsa things ain't what they appear to be." He pointed back the way they'd come, toward the black swirling sky. "That was definitely the wrong way to go. No one lives out that way . . . except Al Gore."

Manny looked surprised. "Al Gore? The ex vice president's here?"

Ned almost laughed. "If I've head that question once, I've heard it a hundred times. Nah, it ain't Clinton's second-in-command. This Al Gore's a crazy psychotic asshole. His real name's Al Gordon, but . . ." Ned shook his head. "Yeah, he's someone you guys need to watch out for. Other than the demons, of course."

"Demons?"

"Hold on, I'll get to the demons shortly. Just watch out for Al, he's a sociopathic devil-worshipping asshole, goes about killing folk for black magic rituals. Sometimes we wake up in the morning and find the headless bodies, other times sometimes folks go missing and all we find are splatters of their blood everywhere." Ned gave a little shiver. "Sometimes he even sends the damn gargoyles to kidnap folks for him." Ned frowned. "Yeah, I know what you're both thinking:

why don't we just send a posse out into the Dark Zone to capture him, right?"

Manny hadn't been thinking that, but he didn't interrupt. What Ned was saying was very enlightening stuff.

"Well, we *did* send posses. Three times, groups of brave men have driven over to the Dark Zone to kill Al Gore. Few of 'em ever came back." He shrugged again. "It's like the bastard's got an early warning—"

"NOOOOOOOOO!" Rick growled then.

Ned and Manny stared at him in surprise. "What's wrong?" Ned asked.

Rick seemed to pick his words with care. "*This* is wrong," he said slowly, his face and shaven head gleaming with sweat, his eyes bright as glowing coals. "This goddam place is wrong." He shook a finger at Ned. "Look here, man—I, for one, ain't buyin' this bullshit you're selling us! We're not in Hell and that's that!"

"Yes, you are," Ned replied simply. "Well, this ain't 'Hell' Hell—this part of it's called SADE, as in Sex, Agony, Detention and Enlightenment. Like I was saying, it's—"

"STOP IT, STOP IT, STOP IT!" Rick yelled at him, his eyes bulging with rage. "THIS AIN'T FUCKING HELL! WE AREN'T DEAD!"

Ned's expression remained calm. "Man, I never said that you were dead. But you're in Hell just the same."

"NO, I AM FUCKING NOT IN HELL! AND NO, FUCKING NO, THERE ARE NO DEMONS WAITING FOR ME DOWN THE DAMN ROAD!" Rick opened the pickup's door and climbed down.

"Hey, where the hell are you going?" Manny called after him.

Rick didn't reply. Instead, he set off across the barren countryside, in the direction of the small shed. They were on the other side of the road from the river; there were no obstructions in his path.

Ned pointed after him. "At least he's headed in the right direction," he informed Manny. "Alright, go after him. Quick, before he reaches that shed."

Manny looked nervously at Ned. "Why? Is there another one of those shadow-things that ate Randy in the shed?"

"What's in there is something even worse than that; but it's something that you two newbies have gotta see." He gave Manny a shove towards the open passenger side door. "Hurry up. That's the reason I parked my truck here. Something you guys gotta see. I know you both think I'm talking BS, so go have a look-see."

Manny leapt down. "Hey, Rick, wait up!" He was about to set off running after his friend, but Ned called him back. "Hey, listen. When you guys get to the shed, push open the door and peek in. But no matter what happens, don't set a foot in there. You get that, man? Don't you *dare* set a foot inside there."

Manny nodded and ran after Rick. He caught up with him ten yards from the shed. Rick was busy muttering to himself about "Crazy rednecks in armored pickup trucks."

Manny quickly explained Ned's instructions, and then they both stepped up to the little shed and opened its door.

The air around them instantly filled with loud screams and other bloodcurdling noises.

The two young men stared into the shed, not even noticing the occasional blasts of heat blowing out of its door. They remained by the shed door for a very long time, with both of their faces growing paler by the moment. Then, not bothering to shut the door, they retreated quickly back to Ned's pickup truck and got in.

Behind them, a scaly green hand dripping with freshly spilled blood pushed the shed door shut again.

In the truck, Manny was speechless. Rick managed to find words: "A pool of fire . . . people burning and screaming . . . flaming prison cells . . . people spitted and roasting like turkeys . . ." Rick stared helplessly at Ned. "You're right, man . . . this *is* Hell."

Manny nodded his silent agreement.

Ned smiled coldly and put the truck in motion. "Yeah, it is, boys. Now, while I drive you into town, you two just relax and listen to the little survival lecture I'm about to give you. It won't take too long, 'cos I gotta go check for other fresh arrivals."

CHAPTER 7

Duncan & Edie

"Hey, screw all these turnoffs," Edie said, pointing at the featureless, sky-high wall of rock ahead. "Let's just drive to either end of the highway and see where it leads. I think there's houses down there."

Duncan nodded, then circled the silver Altima off the road and back onto it again. "It was worth a try," he said as they headed back towards the highway. "Whoever built these turnoffs did so for a reason."

The car seemed to lift as they rode over the river. Edie plugged her nose with fingers against the smell. It was inconceivable to her that a body of water could be this polluted.

"Listen, Duncan," she said patiently as they approached the highway again. "This is the *fourth* turnoff we've so far investigated. It's fair to assume now that they don't lead out of here."

"One of them might."

"No, I don't think any of them do. Wherever this is, it's a crazy place, made by a crazy mind. So it's safe to assume that they'd do crazy things like make roads that lead nowhere."

"Edie, I'm worried that there's something nasty waiting at the end of the highway."

She laughed to cover her own nervousness. "C'mon, baby, don't be silly. You'd prefer if it was the end of the rainbow?" Then she scowled and tapped her fingernails on the dashboard. "But you may be right there. Maybe at the end of the rainbow we'd get a phone signal to call out of here."

Since discovering the oddity of this place, Edie had been trying unsuccessfully to make a phone call. Both she and Duncan's phones showed zero network coverage.

"I think the black sun is blocking the phone signals," Duncan had said once, which Edie found both frightening and perplexing.

Now Duncan frowned. "We'll just check one or two more and then—" *Don't be silly? Seriously?* It had just occurred to him that any one of these deserted turnoffs would be a great location to leave Edie's corpse. Only hitch in that plan was, there didn't seem to be any vultures around here to eat her body after he'd killed her. So far they'd seen no wildlife of any sort. Not even bugs.

"No—I've had enough of going back and forth," Edie said firmly. Then she smiled nicely at him. "Hey, you seem rather grumpy. How 'bout a quickie to calm you down and cheer you up?"

At her suggestion, Duncan felt his penis swelling in his pants. But no, not out here on the highway. And, besides, he hated her. So he shook his head.

"You're sure?" she inquired sweetly.

He nodded. "Yes, I'm sure, baby. This is neither the time nor the place for sex."

She shrugged with some disappointment. "Alright, later then." Then she pouted, which to Duncan's chagrin, made her look impossibly pretty—she had such lovely heart-shaped lips. "C'mon, man," she urged, "so far I've gone along with all your suggestions. How 'bout if we do this my way for a change? So . . . lets just drive off into the sunset, huh?"

"You and your damn romantic associations." But he stopped the car at the intersection and nodded at her. "Alright, girl, pick a side. Left or right?"

"Left," she replied without hesitation. "That's where all the pink is. I kinda fancy seeing a pink sunset."

"Edie, the damn sun is *overhead*. Besides which, it's black and I don't think it sets at all. It hasn't shifted position since we arrived here."

"Man, just drive. Let me worry about that. I can dream, can't I?"

Shrugging, consoling himself that Edith Forrest would soon be dead and then he'd no longer have to put up with her irrational demands and horrible person, Duncan White swerved the silver Nissan left and drove down the highway towards the ominous pink haze.

He didn't drive too fast though. He thought he saw buildings up ahead now and wasn't in any hurry to confront what awaited them there. For all he knew, they could be heading straight towards a pack of horrible and hungry monsters.

Slow and steady stays alive, he figured.

CHAPTER 8

666

"Yeah," Ned explained to his two passengers, "you're still on Route 666, just the crossover version of the highway. Don't ask me how it works, but as far as anyone knows, this road is an exact mile-for-mile and curve-for-curve duplicate of the Ohio one between Zanesville and Dresden."

Ned was driving faster now towards the pink zone of sky, but still not speeding. Rick and Manny were both silent, still trying to come to terms with what they'd seen inside that little shed.

One sharp contrast to the opposite end of the highway was that the houses at this end of Route 666 were all modern American homes. Bungalows, duplexes, and story buildings lined the roadside. Most of the houses looked abandoned and a fair number of them were in evident disrepair, but none seemed to have been constructed later than the last quarter of the last century.

Ned was about to go on with his explanation, but at that very moment, the town signboard came into clear view: "HELLCOME TO 666! POPULATION VARIABLE!" it read, in dripping red letters on a green background.

"Ha ha ha! Just a little joke by the mayor," Ned observed.

"The town's called 666?" Rick asked tiredly. "A town called 666?"

Ned nodded. "Seems the only logical name. Actually, we call this entire underworld 666."

"How long has this place been in existence?"

"I dunno. It was here when I got here."

"Ned, how long have *you* been here?"

Ned lifted a hand from the steering wheel and scratched his bearded chin. " 'Bout eleven years, give or take a few." He nodded.

"Yeah, it may very well be more or less years than that. At times time seems variable and unreliable here."

Manny gaped. "Eleven frigging years?"

Ned smiled sadly. "Yep. Been trying to get out ever since, but—and this is a point I'm tryin' to get across to you guys—there's apparently no way out of this damn place." He shook his head. "Not that I really believe that, but"—he gestured up over the passing houses, at the rock walls enclosing the desert countryside—"I've been looking for an escape route for eleven years and ain't found one yet."

"How'd you get here, man?"

"Same way you did . . . same way everyone else here did. Me and the wife were driving up from Jackson, Tennessee to the little town of Sugarcreek in Ohio. About halfway along Route 666 we turned into a gas station to fill up—the Red Eagle it was called—and bang, next thing we know, we're stuck here between these goddamned walls of mountains and the black and pink end points."

"What lies beyond the pink and black at the end of the road?"

Ned shrugged and his bearded face took on an expression of intense misery. "Nothing, guys. Nothing. I hate this frigging place and . . ."

But they'd arrived fully in town now and so Ned Shriver kept quiet. He pulled the GMC pickup truck to the side of the road and parked.

"Alright, boys, this is where you get down." He pointed ahead, down the highway. "Keep on following the road, and turn left after the Watkins drugstore. Town hall's straight ahead then. They'll be having a welcoming meeting for newbies."

Rick and Manny got out of the pickup truck. "Thanks, Ned," Manny said. "We really appreciate your saving us back there."

Rick nodded. "Yeah, we do."

"Think nothing of it. Just sorry I couldn't have arrived in time to save your brother. Alright, time for me to go see if anyone else needs my help."

Ned U-turned the pickup truck, then called from the other side of the road, "So, I'll see you two around. Say 'Hi' to the mayor for me!"

Then he was driving off in a cloud of exhaust smoke.

Rick and Manny watched him go for a while, then they looked around at their surroundings.

Unlike the Dark Zone where the gargoyles had attacked them, this place showed clear signs of human occupation. In addition to being of more recent design, the houses were well maintained, with drapes fluttering in open windows and laundry hanging on washing lines. There were garbage cans out front of the houses and cars parked in a few garages. A white cat paced along a roof. They saw several shops, though none appeared open. There was even a traffic light at the intersection ahead, though it seemed busted, and there were no power lines overhead. Even the sidewalk looked normal, cracked concrete and all.

Rick read a storefront sign—"Melvin's Barbershop, No. 49 Route 666"—then spat on the sidewalk. "666? What a dumb name."

Manny nodded. "Yeah, but this place looks more livable than the other end of the road. Even if the sky *is* as pink as a whore's pussy." He pointed up, over a nearby blue bungalow. "Except for these two walls of rock behind everything, we could be hitchhikers arriving in just about any small North American town."

Rick looked around at the houses then nodded. "Alright, but where is everyone? This whole place seems deserted."

"They're most likely at the town meeting Ned mentioned, waiting for us."

They set off in the direction Ned had indicated, with Rick asking, "Manny, do you really believe all Ned told us? I mean, 'bout this place being Hell?"

Manny shrugged. "You saw what I saw, dude. And Cody and your brother are both dead now, killed by stuff I never even saw in the movies." He shook his head at his companion's questioning face. "So, if the facts fit . . . at least until we find a better explanation for where we are."

"Shit, Randy's dead, man," Rick wept as they walked along. "My little brother's dead, man."

Manny couldn't think of an adequate response to that, so he kept quiet.

CHAPTER 9

Duncan & Edie

Almost arriving in town, Duncan and Edie met a man in a black pickup truck. He was turning out of a small compound a short distance after the creepy "HELLCOME TO 666! POPULATION VARIABLE!" town sign. He introduced himself as Ned Shriver and was friendly enough, but was in a hurry. He gave them directions to the town hall, then sped off the other way.

Edie burst into tears as Ned drove off. "It's such a relief to see a human face here!" she wept on Duncan's shoulder.

Duncan had forgotten that she could be emotional like this. He was still going to kill her though. Nothing would change that.

When they arrived at the 666 town hall, they found the welcoming meeting already underway, with the town mayor—a busty middle-aged brunette—explaining to seven other befuddled fresh arrivals where they were now and how life functioned in 666.

The town hall was packed full of people. There were no electric lights on, but the windows were open, so everything was clear to the eye.

On their entering the hall, a Chinese lady usher named May Wong greeted them and escorted them to reserved seats at the front of the hall. As she showed them forward, she quickly filled them in on a few details. For instance, she told them the mayor's name was Sally Thornwood.

The other seven fresh arrivals were everyday folks too—a man and his pregnant wife, two young men (one of whom had a shaven head), a biker couple, and a white-haired man in his sixties, whom they later discovered was a dentist. The dentist's face was bleeding from what seemed to be claw marks. The man with the pregnant wife was also hurt, his left arm being bandaged by a nurse while the meeting proceeded.

The lady usher had told Duncan and Edie that the man standing beside Sally Thornwood on the podium was Sheriff Hook. Sheriff Hook was dark and muscular and had a goatee. His name clearly came from the metal hook he had in place of his right hand. The sheriff was dressed in a blue uniform shirt over black trousers.

"So, that's how it goes, folks," Sally Thornwood said in her lush southern drawl. "Y'all stuck down here in 666 for life." She gestured to her companion. "Or, like our good lawman Hookie likes to put it— you may consider this as life imprisonment."

The white-haired dentist raised his hand. "I have a question, ma'am."

"Ask away, sir."

"Are you absolutely certain that there's no way out?"

"None whatsoever," the brunette mayor promptly replied, her white dress tightening around her impressive bosom. "We've tried just about every damn thing you can imagine without success, even drilling into the mountains." She sighed. "Total waste of time. Once we leave off for the night, the rock face reforms itself; by morning it's like we never set a pick or drill to it."

The dentist nodded. Sally Thornwood went on with her welcome speech:

"Don't y'all worry though. There's lots of food and liquor, though it all tastes like shit, and seeing as the lot of ya are already in Hell anyway, you don't need to worry about God punishing ya for your sins."

This got a loud cheer from the old-timers. Duncan had by now estimated that there were about sixty people in the hall. From teenagers to men and women in their seventies. No children. And, except for the just-arrived lady, there were no pregnant women in the hall either.

"So have fun," Sally Thornwood said. "If you need a vehicle, head over to the used-car lot and pick one up for a token cost. Find a job ya like to do an' do it. Just don't mess with other folks' personal space and property." She smirked. "I mean it. There's lots of guns and ammo in our gun shop and just about everyone here's armed because of Al Gore, so watch ya—"

"Al Gore?" the male biker asked. "The ex vice president's here?"

"Not that one," the lady mayor replied. "We got our own serial-killer version. Sonofabitch is worse than one of the goddamn demons. You gotta watch out for him, or he'll abduct and butcher you."

The pregnant woman began weeping.

Seeing this, Sheriff Hook whispered to the mayor and she stepped back from the lectern so he could address the crowd:

"Now, now," the sheriff said, "there's no *real* need to get alarmed, lady. We haven't lost anyone from around here in the past month. Al lives out in the Dark Zone with the damn gargoyles . . . hardly ever drives down this way nowadays, 'cos he realizes we're all watching for him. All you all need to do is visit the gun shop tomorrow and arm yourselves—we've got everything here, from rifles and shotguns to little concealed-carry weapons for you girls. That way if Al attempts to surprise you—you'll have a surprise of your own for him too."

CHAPTER 10

Rick & Manny

Rick ran a hand over his shaved head, then whispered to his companion, "Manny, just listen to this sheriff guy. This is getting crazier by the moment."

Manny nodded. "Like the old Wild West, yeah? Soon, he's gonna be telling us about the local brothel and salon."

Sheriff Hook had noticed the two conversing. "Now listen up, boys. Yeah, sure, this place is Hell, but we believe in maintaining decency and law and order here. As you must've understood from what I've been saying so far, all the ladies 'round here are armed and dangerous, so watch your step. If you get shot, you get shot."

Manny protested: "Hey—we don't plan on—!"

The sheriff interrupted him with a scowl and a wave of his hook-hand. "That's good to know. If your libidinous urges come over you, and you ain't found yourself a girlfriend yet and don't feel like jerking off either, we've plenty of hookers around here too. You can hire one of those. But don't you dare attempt any raping, or I'll personally slice your damn balls off."

"And we'll send the rest of your rapist ass out for Al Gore to play with!" a woman yelled from the back of the hall.

This set off a whole lot of laughter.

"Yeah, yeah, sure, dude," Rick replied the sheriff. "Don't lose your other hand over it."

This provoked yet more laughter.

Sheriff Hook stared as meanly as he could at the two young upstarts and then, apparently imagining he'd put sufficient of the fear of God (or of Satan) into them, stepped back from the lectern again.

CHAPTER 11

Duncan & Edie

Duncan looked around at the gathering, then at Edie. "Do you believe this?" he whispered.

She squeezed his arm. "Baby, I'd *love* not to believe it. But what else can I believe?"

The mayor was speaking again: "Alright, everyone, now onto accommodations. Lots of the houses are empty. Pick any of those that you like and move in. But that's for tomorrow. Tonight—I'm using that figuratively, of course; though the clocks work, the damn sun never sets, so there's no real division between the days . . . What I wanna say is, for the moment, 'fore you find yourselves suitable accommodations, y'all can find lodgings at the hotel down the road. Place is called the Hellton. Lotsa empty rooms . . . just don't pick any room numbered with a six. So, no Room Six, or Room Sixteen, or Sixty-One—if ya understand me. Same goes for houses too. Don't try to move into any of those with a six in its number, or else . . ."

A pale hand raised, Sally Thornwood let the warning hang like a threat.

Duncan gulped. "I think we're fucked," he whispered to Edie.

She giggled. "We're gonna fuck anyway."

"Is sex all you think about?"

She shrugged. "If we're really trapped here, it'll be a welcome distraction."

"And watch out for the demons," Mayor Thornwood said.

"Demons?" the pregnant woman asked, shuddering. "Demons?"

"Yeah, demons," the mayor replied. "Though this ain't the *real* Hell—I mean, we clearly ain't roasting forever here—still, the infernals have access to us." She frowned. "They're a nuisance, for sure; always dangerous and sometimes deadly." She scowled at her

39

questioner. "Lady, being pregnant, you need to be extra-careful. The fiends may try to eat your baby."

The pregnant woman promptly fainted in her seat. Her husband, his arm freshly bandaged, looked helplessly up at the mayor, then bent and tried to revive his wife.

"Well that's about everything for tonight," Sally Thornwood said. "Other horrors to watch for are the 'goyles and the shadow-things, but we can discuss those later." She smiled. "Welcome to 666, everyone. Hope y'all survive this place."

CHAPTER 12

Rick & Manny . . . Settling In

That was the end of the meeting. As it broke up, the townsfolk came over to greet the new arrivals.

Most of the townspeople seemed healthy. Truth be told, no one in the hall seemed exactly happy; each face had a look of resignation to an inevitable fate etched into it.

The numbers of men and women who'd attended were about equal, with the highest age concentration being in the twenty-five to forty age range. The three or four teens in attendance had come with their parents. Most of the townsfolk were Caucasian, but there were eight or so Negroes present too, some Native Americans, four or five Asians, and several Latino couples.

***

After the crowd had dispersed a bit, Rick and Manny relayed Ned's greetings to the mayor. Then they shuffled out of the hall after May Wong, the Chinese lady who'd shown them to their seats.

May was now escorting the newbies down the road to the Hellton Hotel.

Having lost their own car, Rick and Manny hitched a ride with the young couple who'd arrived right after them, a hot blonde and her boyfriend who had a silver Nissan Altima. Their guide May was getting into the car ahead of theirs, a white Mercedes S-Class which belonged to the white-haired dentist. The biker couple were already rolling out of the parking lot on their Harley Davidson and heading downtown towards the hotel. The other just-arrived vehicle—which had blood smears on its windshield and was missing its driver's door—was waiting to follow the convoy.

Once Rick and Manny were seated in the back of the Altima, the blonde turned around to make conversation: "I don't know about you guys," she said, "but finding myself here is too damn creepy to figure out. It's like a nightmare. I'm praying I'll wake up soon."

Her boyfriend, a grim fellow who was focused on following the white car ahead of them, now scowled. "Yeah, this is a nightmare alright."

Rick had fallen silent again. Manny agreed with the blonde girl: "You're right. All I can think about now is falling sleep and waking up back in the real world."

She nodded and gestured outside at the houses they were passing. "If all this is a hallucination, it's the best one ever. This almost looks like my hometown."

"Well, here we are, guys," her boyfriend said then, bringing the car to a halt.

The four of them got out of the car and followed May and the others into the Hellton Hotel, which, apart from its grandiose name, looked like any small town hotel: a long white three-story building with an extensive parking lot, balconies on each floor and an awning over the front entrance. Large knobby cacti grew around the place.

There was no receptionist in the hotel lobby. Prompted by May, everyone split up to look for empty rooms.

"Most are unoccupied at the moment, so any floor and door you like!" she called as they headed off. "You'll either find the keys in the locks, or hanging on a nail on the door. Just avoid any door with a six in its number."

"Hey, why's that?" the grizzly-looking biker asked, one muscular arm around his woman's shoulder. "I mean, the mayor warned us about that too, so what's the deal there?"

With a murmur of agreement, everyone turned back to hear May's reply to his question.

The Chinese woman explained: "Most 'six' doors are 'trapdoors'— as in they contain actual traps. Some don't actually open into rooms at all. Others do, but you'll still be in danger."

"Hey, enlighten us, lady. What kinda danger you talking 'bout?" the biker asked.

May tapped the receptionist's bell for emphasis. "Okay, most 'six' doors have stuff behind them that can kill you. Stuff like bottomless holes in their floors, shadow-things and sentient furnaces; even hidden wall pits or ventilation shafts full of flesh-eating maggots. So, just stay clear of them and stay safe. You don't want to wake up in the morning and find your beds full of hungry grubs, do you?"

"I don't know what shadow-things are," the dentist said, "but sentient furnaces and a bed full of flesh-eating maggots sounds bad enough to me."

The biker nodded sagely. His lady, however, looked about to throw up. The pregnant lady still seemed too dazed from her previous faint to have clearly heard what May had just said. Her husband looked almost as out of it as she did.

"So alright, go pick your lodgings, everyone," May encouraged. "And when you're satisfied with your rooms, come back downstairs for dinner." After ringing the receptionist's buzzer again to get everyone's attention, she pointed to the large hallway that led out to the rear of the hotel. "The restaurant's out back by the swimming pool. It'll be open till 2 a.m., which is general closing time around here."

Everyone nodded and resumed dispersing.

"Let's check out the ground level rooms," Manny suggested to Rick. "I don't feel like climbing the stairs."

Rick grunted a reply.

"Hey, so we'll be seeing you guys around then," the blonde said. "Oh, sorry, we forgot to introduce ourselves. "I'm Edie and this is Duncan."

"Rick and Manny."

"Delighted," Duncan said.

"Maybe we'll see each other tomorrow," Edie said, then pointed overhead at the balconies. "We're heading upstairs. I expect we'll be rooming on the second floor . . . somewhere in the middle. I like looking over balconies in the morning." She took her boyfriend's arm and pulled him away.

"They're a weird pair," Manny said as he watched them head for the stairs.

"Huh? Who?" Rick asked over his shoulder. He was already heading down the walkway that connected the hotel lobby to the ground floor rooms.

Manny hurried after him. "Those two—Edie and Duncan—they're a strange couple. Not her though, she's cool. But there's a look in her boyfriend's eyes like he can't stand her."

Rick shrugged. "Can't stand her? Then what the hell are they doing dating each other?"

Manny pondered that for a few moments and then he and Rick began checking out the hotel rooms. The first two rooms were trashed, but Room 3 was in good condition. The sound of voices from Room 4 told them it was occupied, so they moved into Room 3.

CHAPTER 13

Slick, Pearl & Minx

"Girls, some *boys* just moved in next door," Slick Rogers announced, leaning back inside the window and taking a drag on his joint.

Slick Rogers was a small, handsome fellow with long brown hair. He was addressing his two female roommates: Pearl Harbor and Minx Fortune. Pearl was tall, had long black hair and large breasts; while Minx was a short redhead with small breasts and a large mean streak.

Slick, Pearl and Minx were all in their mid-twenties.

The three of them were also part of 666's force of sex workers.

"Young and good-looking dudes too," Slick went on. "You two are gonna love 'em."

Pearl lifted her eyes from her novel. "We can hear them too, baby."

"Yeah, that we can," Minx agreed, looking up from painting her toenails black. "It's the sixth of June today, and a short while ago it was six p.m. . . . so we'll have new arrivals in 666." Then she laughed. "But I know, you just can't wait to suck their dicks, can you, Pearl?"

"Only for cash, hon," Pearl retorted, waving her book in the air. "My upper and lower lips only spread for bread."

Slick crossed the room and sat on the couch. "I hate all this cryptic, mystic . . . satanic . . . bullshit. That's why I never like attending the welcoming party at town hall—it depresses me."

Pearl shrugged. "It's the shit-stem, man. We're trapped in it, might as well get used to it, you know?"

"As in, we're like—fucked," Minx said. "Though, I gotta agree with you on that point, man—no way did I wanna be there tonight to see all those scared new arrivals. I'd just be reminding myself of how fucked we are down here."

"No, we're the ones doing all the fucking," Pearl retorted. "And, we get to pick and choose who we fuck."

Minx laughed. "Baby doll, I didn't see you hurrying off to welcome anyone, did I?"

Pearl didn't reply.

Slick sucked on his joint a little longer, then said: "Pearl, honey, how 'bout you drop that book of yours and come help me unwind with a blowjob?"

She considered the request for a moment, then nodded. "Alright, but only if you eat me too afterwards. Turnaround's fair play. Deal?"

"Deal." Slick slid off his shorts and waited with stiff penis in hand.

Pearl stuck a bookmark in her romance novel, then slipped off her bra and walked over to him. He spread his legs. She sat between them and took his member in her mouth, playing her tongue up and down its rigid length. Slick relaxed back and let her work on him. After a while, he began moaning with pleasure.

Minx looked up once, smirked at them both, and resumed painting her toenails.

After a few minutes Slick came in Pearl's mouth. She swallowed, licked her lips clean, then tapped him on the thigh. "Alright, switch places, my turn."

"Nah," he gasped.

She frowned. "Dude, you promised."

He squirmed down on the couch. "Sit on my face and I'll eat you."

She positioned her crotch over his head, then gasped when he dug his tongue into her dripping sex. She gripped his head firmly and rubbed his mouth against her vagina. He licked her, squeezing her ass with both hands while doing so.

After her orgasm, Pearl slid down Slick's body and lay on him panting.

"Yeah, that was good," she gasped. "I feel better able cope with life's shit now."

***

'Slick' wasn't Slick's real name, any more than Pearl Harbor or Minx Fortune were the girls' names. But they were sex workers and aliases were in.

Slick had been in 666 for five years now, after making the same mistake as everyone else here, of stopping to buy gas at the Red Eagle between Zanesville and Dresden, in the evening on the 6th of June.

Before arriving down here Slick had worked in Burger King. Minx had been a college student. Pearl had been working at Starbucks. Here, all three of them had discovered a latent interest in profitable promiscuity and had joined the world's oldest profession.

Pearl Harbor was a bit of a stoner, an easy-going young woman. She accepted each day as it came and tried to make the best of it. She had no doubts that she was stuck here for good, so she spent her days and nights having fun.

Minx on the other hand, was very hyper. She was impatient, bitchy and had a mean streak a mile wide.

No one really blamed Minx for her occasional nastiness though. Five months ago, Minx had unwisely followed a guy named Roland Smith down the highway to go have sex in the church graveyard.

They never made it there. Al Gore had captured them both and borne them off to his evil lair in the Dark Zone. Roland, he'd instantly butchered. Minx, however, he'd kept alive for sexual perversions.

Minx had escaped from Al a week later. Bleeding from deep cuts all over her body, she'd stumbled out into the highway while Ned had been driving by and collapsed right in front of his truck. Ned had first thought she was dead—she'd been that badly slashed up, with one wound so deep he could see her guts in the cut. He'd brought the raving, tormented girl back into town.

Minx had complete amnesia as to how she'd gotten away from the psychopathic Al. Her memory loss was almost total—she'd been unable to remember a single thing beyond her hooker name 'Minx.'

Her previous life was still completely lost to her. Her physical wounds were long healed, but the past was still a locked door to the former college student, her 'memories' of it reconstructed from what Slick and Pearl had told her.

Every now and again, Minx, gun in handbag, would stalk off for days, riding a motorbike out of town to camp in the houses near the old church. She'd claim she just wanted to clear her head, but everyone knew the truth: Minx was waiting for Al Gore to drive past on one of his raids into town so she could ambush him and shoot him dead.

They all wished her luck. But the 666 townsfolk all expected Minx to soon go missing again, and for good this time.

***

Minx finally decided her toenails looked okay. After putting the bottle of black nail paint away, she checked the time on her watch, then said: "Hey, guys, it's nine frigging p.m. So, what're we gonna do tonight? Introduce ourselves to the neighbor boys and see if they wanna play?"

Pearl leaned up on Slick's chest. "Hey, that's a cool idea!"

However, Slick shook his head. "Not tonight, ladies. I assure you that right now, those two guys next door are too confused and scared to think of fucking—even if you two hot bitches were both Miss Universe you couldn't get a shared boner out of the two of 'em."

"What then?"

"We'll wait till morning, then you can be sure they'll need comforting in a big way."

Minx's face creased up unpleasantly. "And tonight? Are we three just gonna sit in here and drown in sad reflections? Maybe you two are both fine now that you've eaten each other, but I want some sex tonight."

Slick pushed Pearl off him and sat up. "Get dressed, girls. We'll drive down to Fat Larry's bar. There's certain to be lots of action there for both of you fine young whores." He grinned, rising to his feet and shuffling over to the closet, where he began picking out clothes. "That hot waitress Lucy might even be in need of my bedroom services again."

Minx nodded her agreement, but then she held up a hand. "Wait a bit. My nails need to dry first."

CHAPTER 14

Sex Sex Sex & Religion

In 666, sex was the number one pastime. Folks still acted with decency—Mayor Thornwood and Sheriff Hook insisted on that—but behind closed doors, everyone did what they liked, with few regrets.

With no children in 666, there were no morality laws.

Those Christians who'd found themselves trapped here had quickly become convinced that God was punishing them for some sin they'd overlooked, and while not exactly ditching their faith, had realized they had nothing to lose by becoming as hedonistic as anyone else.

All except for Reverend Stevens, that was . . .

This casting off of moral restraints applied to those of other religions also. Once one believed in life after death (or even in reincarnation), finding oneself in Hell (or lower down the astral scale that one thought one should be) merely confirmed one's beliefs as true.

Ironically, those worst affected by the new order of things weren't the religious, but the atheists, most of whom had spent so much mental time convincing themselves of God's non-existence that they'd forgotten there might be a Devil waiting somewhere; and whom, now that they'd found themselves trapped alive in a realm outside of man's knowledge of time and space, and one populated with fiends to boot, generally felt like the universe had conspired to shit on them.

Some years, more men than women arrived in 666. Other years it was the reverse case.

Each time a man died, like all the ones who'd gone hunting Al Gore—the town ended up with surplus womenfolk. Someone had to emotionally cater for the grieving girlfriends and widows. Also, when women died (which tended to be a rarer occurrence here), there were the widowers to look after.

Then there were all the single men and women too. Someone had to be responsible for easing sexual tensions among the 666 citizenry, or else there were certain to be endless jealousies developing and, in a place with lots of guns and no gun-control laws, a whole lot of 'crime of passion' murders.

Which would just result in further reductions to an already small and only once-a-year restocked population.

So here in 666, the prostitutes performed an essential function, and were respected and paid like everyone else.

CHAPTER 15

Ned

Ned Shriver keep his eyes peeled while heading into the Dark Zone. By now, he'd been up here so many times that caution was second nature to him. He'd been ushering in the new arrivals for five years now, ever since the previous guy had been eaten by a shadow-thing.

Ned was a bit of a loner. He didn't live in town with the others, and didn't share their sense of fatalism, or their descent into hedonism either. As much as it was possible for a person to have principles here, he was trying to have some.

Yeah, it's always like this every sixth of June, he thought while steering his reinforced black truck down the highway, *you save some and you lose some. I hate losin' folks, but it can't be helped. There's only one frigging one of me—everyone's too damn scared to leave town tonight—and I can't be everywhere at once.*

By Ned's calculations, there should be two more arrivals tonight. He did the math again: *Five in the hall, before those two I rescued from the 'goyles, and those guys said two of their friends were killed. Then the guy and girl in the silver car. That's eleven so far, and the usual quota we get on the sixth is either six or thirteen people. So there should be two more folks out here.*

He'd arrived in the Dark Zone now; was well in amongst the old gothic ruins. He pulled up near the young men's destroyed SUV, reversing his GMC truck up over the sidewalk and parking it at ninety-degrees to the road, so he could see both ways down the highway at a glance.

Twenty feet away from him lay a mess of scattered red bones—one of the kid's remains. Before shutting off his engine Ned instinctively looked outwards at the roofs of the nearby buildings. The gargoyles were wary of him now—the way he'd reinforced his truck, dive-bombing it just shattered their skulls—but one or two of them might be hungry enough to dare his shotgun.

The roofs were clear of gargoyles. Ned leaned his shotgun on the steering wheel and checked his wristwatch. Like all others here in 666, it ran on old-time wind-up technology and had a large 24-hour dial that was split into a black and a white half, each of those in turn being partitioned into twelve instead of six. With the sun never setting here and time as fluid as water, the idea behind the black/white dial was to let the wearer know at a glance if it was 'day' or 'night.' Wall clocks were the same, and there were lots of big town clocks that one could learn the time from. The timepieces all had a huge '6' at the top, indicating 6 a.m., and another at the bottom, indicating 6 p.m.

At the moment it was 10 in the black. 10 p.m. here, that was. Back in the human world it was still a few minutes past six.

The 'portal' which sucked folks off Ohio's Route 666 and transferred them down into this underworld remained open for just six minutes up there. Those six minutes however somehow stretched out to six hours here. So Ned would be expecting folks for two hours more.

Once it's midnight—midnight where there's never any darkness?—I'll drive back home and catch me some sleep.

Ned waited, occasionally looking in his rearview mirror, just in case some of the gargoyles got stupid enough to take him on. He peered left and right down Route 666, expecting those abrupt electric flashes that announced a new transition.

"This place is the utter pits," he grumbled to himself after a while. "And the sooner I can find the exit from here—the sooner I'll be gone. And I sure as hell won't miss it. Eleven goddamn years searching! She-it!"

Ned tapped the barrel of his shotgun. This place—this entire underworld life—was a million miles away from his previous existence as a carpet salesman in Jackson, Tennessee. Back then, he'd been well-liked at work and by his friends. He'd been moderately successful and had led a comfortable life. Yes, back then Ned Shriver's only worries had been his 14-year-old son Kenny's burgeoning teenage rebellion and his wife's sudden interest in kinky sex—whips, handcuffs, and such deviant like.

Ned had no interest in all that leather and bondage nonsense.

And now . . . here in 666? His wife could whip and be whipped to her heart's content. So they'd split up . . . Nancy Shriver now ran one of the local sex shops.

Ned had a theory concerning why everyone here was preoccupied with sex to some degree. He was certain the colored extremes of the road subtly affected folk's minds once they were a certain distance from it.

Take the town 666, for instance. It was built less than a mile from the pink end, which according to the demons, was the boundary with Hell's 'Sex' zone. (The demons actually called this whole outpost region SADE, like that ancient Frenchman's name.) This other end of the highway—and the warped antique town here—was even closer situated to Hell's 'Agony' zone. And this was where that asshole Al Gore and the damn gargoyles—those hellish masses of flying appetite—all hung out. This end of Route 666 was also where there was the highest concentration of shadow-things and other unholy fuck-ups that could terminate one's life in the blink of an eye.

In the blink of an eye. The thought made Ned grip his shotgun harder. *Dammit, I'm letting this place get to me!*

After a while Ned got bored with sitting so long in one place. He started the pickup truck up again, and headed back towards town. He went slowly. The road was only 14.7 miles long, no point speeding.

***

Keeping his eyes peeled for that telltale electric flash, Ned pondered his surroundings some more:

The black sun; the seemingly mile-high sheer mountainsides; the barren two-mile-wide plain with its useless spiky cacti; the oily duplicate Muskingum River, with its damn stinkfish and other horrible residents. (The river's oily surface reflected the sun in a very creepy way.) And the two towns.

He pondered how organized it all was.

Here, for sure, there was a definite method to the madness.

All these years later, Ned still wasn't certain who ran this place. At one point, he'd been sure it was the Devil, but then demons were rarely seen here. They could and did visit from time to time, but not much. But then again, this definitely wasn't Heaven or its environs.

He stared at his shotgun—a pump-action with no model name or serial number. It however worked better than any shotgun he'd ever owned back home.

Who filled the stores with stuff? Like this shotgun, for instance, and the box of spare shells sitting on the dashboard? It didn't matter what the commodity was, the stores in town never ran out of stock. No matter how much was used up each day, each night it got replenished. Just like the 666 gas stations never ran out of gas or diesel either.

But who replaced the stuff? Ned didn't know.

***

Ned was approaching 666 when he saw the flash. It was on his left, just before the first house and down beside the river.

The transition happening off the road meant that the new arrival was on foot. This generally happened when a person travelling from Dresden to Zanesville parked their car on the shoulder opposite the Red Eagle gas station and crossed the road on foot to the convenience store. If whatever they bought had metal in it (of if they were making a call on their cellphone), they'd wind up *here* on their way back to their car.

Carrying his shotgun, Ned got down from his truck and went to meet the newcomer. He hurried, conscious of the dangers involved; unwilling to lose more people tonight.

The new arrival was a woman in her thirties. Ned found her standing near the riverbank, staring in confusion at the distant mountain wall. She turned on hearing him approach. She had short black hair, gray eyes and was wearing a buttoned-up fur coat that reached down to her boots, as if the weather on Earth had been chilly when she'd transitioned.

Maybe she was heading to a party and only has skimpy clothes on underneath, Ned thought with some amusement.

"Where am I?" the woman asked, her expression perplexed and frightened. "Where on earth is this place?" As expected, she looked dazed. Ned's heart went out to her. She was pretty too.

Seeing as Ned didn't hang around town much, he hadn't been with a woman in quite a while. He suddenly realized he had an erection.

The woman noticed the swollen front of his jeans too. Instead of being offended, her look of fear instantly turned to one of lust.

"Hi, Ned!" she said saucily, pulling her coat open in a quick motion. "Would you like to fuck me?"

Ned moved just in time, dropping to the floor and rolling sideways as six or seven black tentacles shot out of the woman's body at him. Their razor-sharp tips glinted and slashed the air where he'd been standing.

Oops! She's a demon!

While scrambling back to his feet, Ned had a quick look around. The mutilated corpse of the actual new arrival lay behind a rock, in a mess of bloody sand. The dead woman lay on top of her own extracted intestines. All the skin had been peeled off her back and lay in a bloody sheet a short distance from her. The white ridge of her spine was visible, with her ribs jutting from it. Her liver was halfway out of her body. It appeared to have been gnawed on.

Meanwhile, the demon woman was laughing, a foot-long tongue dangling from her mouth between long fangs. Her tentacles retracted back into her body and shot out again, this time shattering a rock when Ned got out of their way for a second time.

Ned considered shooting the demoness, but then decided it would be a waste of ammo. Instead he legged it fast out of there.

All the way back to his truck, the demoness' shrill laugher dogged him. "Come back and fuck me, Ned Shriver!" she mocked. "I'll eat you afterwards, but before then, we'll have a hell of a good time. I'll really make it worth your while, baby!"

Screw this! Ned thought, gunning up the pickup truck, then pulling a quick U-turn and heading back towards the Dark Zone. *One dead, one to go!*

While speeding away, he checked his watch. Just 10:30. Still an hour and a half to wait for that final straggler.

CHAPTER 16

Duncan & Edie

Duncan and Edie chose Room 24 on the Hellton's second floor. The room was spacious and cream-colored. It had a double-bed and a long brown couch, a coffee table, a large wardrobe, and an above average-sized bathroom. There was no telephone, TV, or fridge. The face of the wall clock was split into twenty-four time divisions. The left half of the clock-face was colored black and had a sickle moon painted on.

There were no bulbs or light switches. All light filtered in through the gauzy translucent window drapes.

While Duncan fetched their suitcases, Edie studied the town from the balcony. She frowned at the array of houses, all normal enough on their own, but rendered unwholesome by that endless mountain wall in the background. The town of 666 seemed like a toy town stored in a cardboard box.

Downstairs, several others were also getting things out of their cars.

Looking right up, here the sky did had a soothing pink tint to it, but the gray unscalable cliff faces were a forbidding sight that filled Edie with foreboding. She instinctively knew that this wasn't any kind of a good place.

"Ugh, what a shithole," she groaned with deep feeling. "And we're trapped here?"

"I still hate to believe that that's the truth," Duncan said, joining her by the door. "But I'm prepared to accept that possibility until morning."

Scared by her own question, Edie followed him into their room.

Duncan watched Edie unpack their things. He let her work. He still intended killing her. Now he had additional motivation for the murder:

It's her fault that we're here now, he thought. Then he grudgingly admitted. *Nah, it's my fault, or at least both of ours.*

***

For two years now, Duncan White had been embezzling funds at Cashstretch, the retail chain he worked for. Duncan was in charge of the company's Ohio accounts—diverting the money was easy. The difficulty was in not getting caught.

Duncan's theft had started innocently enough. As an exercise to upgrade his employer's financial security, Duncan had pondered a safe way to steal Cashstretch's money. He'd finally hit on the idea of setting up a dummy company, one he then paid for services it didn't provide. He'd tried it out. Step by step, he'd overcome all the possible hurdles of anyone tracing where the money was being diverted to.

So finally, Duncan had a working theft model and nothing to do with it.

So he'd decided "Why not?" and begun leeching the company's funds for himself.

Duncan was greedy, but not overly so. In the past two years, he'd only stolen half a million dollars. He could have taken thrice as much, but he'd figured caution was his best friend.

But then Edie Forrest, Duncan's assistant, had found out about his stealing.

Duncan's embezzling had escaped even the auditors' notices. But Edie, going through the company's financial records one wet week early in the spring when Duncan had had the flu, had noted the discrepancies.

Edie spent the rest of her boss's sick leave compiling the evidence. When he returned to the office, she confronted him with the proof of his pilfering.

Duncan was stumped. Staring jail-time in the face, all he could do was ask Edie what she wanted. She clearly wanted something, or else it would be the police here in his office now, not herself.

She'd gotten up from her chair and sat on the edge of his desk. "I want half," she'd said, leaning forward and taking hold of his gray tie and tugging symbolically on it, as though it were a leash attached to a collar around his neck. "I want half of everything you've stolen to date and half of all future takings."

Curling the end of his tie between her slim fingers, she let Duncan muse on that for a few moments, then added: "And from now on, we up the take. You're a genius, man—I'd never have figured out this swindle. All that money going into charity payments and also . . . Point is, no one will notice if we take three times as much."

"I . . . we'll . . . get caught," he'd pointed out, already accepting her as a partner in his fraudulent venture, knowing he had no choice but to comply with her demands.

"*You* didn't get caught." She let go of his tie, rearranged her blonde hair.

"Because I didn't take *that much*. Besides, you found out, didn't you? If we take more . . ."

"*Me* finding out doesn't count." She got up, paced round the desk, and wound up sitting on his lap. "Don't worry about it, *darling*," she told him. "No one'll ever discover what's going on. While you were at home I fixed your mistakes in the system. The swindle's foolproof now."

He nodded, wishing she'd get off his lap. Even in this crisis, she was giving him an erection.

Then she'd licked her lips and said, "Of course, we fuck to seal the deal?"

"Huh?" This was completely unexpected. "C'mon, Edie, you're friends with Cheryl." Cheryl Dawson was Duncan's girlfriend.

"She won't miss you for a weekend or two," was Edie's cold reply. "I always feel business partners should be bedroom partners too; it helps them understand each other better." She wriggled her behind on Duncan's lap, then kissed him on the lips. "Your cock seems to agree with me. If this was lunchtime, I'd suck you off—but someone might come in now."

She got off his lap and adjusted her dress. "So, next weekend, baby. You pick the time and place and I'll pack a suitcase."

She blew him a kiss, then blew out of his office. She left Duncan both sexually aroused and totally confused.

Why the hell does she want me? he wondered. While not a slut, Edie Forrest had a lot of male attention in the office.

But Edie clearly did want Duncan. Maybe she wanted him as a trophy; maybe she wanted to power-trip on him; or maybe, like she'd said, she merely wanted to seal the deal. But she meant to have him in her bed.

Duncan knew Edie had his balls in her purse now. He had to play along with her demands.

But he wouldn't do so forever. He couldn't. There was nothing to stop Edie from carelessly getting them both caught; or becoming unreasonable and deciding she wanted the lioness' share for herself; or even denouncing him to management just to take over his job.

These worries had set Duncan to thinking. And after a while, he'd come to a conclusion: If Edie Forrest suddenly went missing, all of his worries were certain to vanish along with her.

After that, while Duncan told Edie he was looking for a nice motel where they'd have lots of privacy, the real focus of his search became to locate a place where he could dump her corpse and expect it never to be found.

He'd not found a good place. He'd however found something much better:

See, Duncan had an uncle named Vince Collins. Uncle Vince lived in Dresden. Uncle Vince was a gangster; was waist deep in the New England/North Central US drug trade. Uncle Vince had agreed to help Duncan dispose of Edie Forrest. All Duncan had to do was drive her up to Dresden, drug her unconscious, and give him a call.

Duncan, however, wanted some payback on Edie for putting him to all this bother and expense—Uncle Vince had said it would cost him a hundred thousand dollars to make her completely disappear.

And since Edie would be disappearing anyway, Duncan had figured it didn't matter if he delivered her to his uncle's goons dead or alive, or in little pieces.

So, in addition to the hunting knife, he'd purchased a thick tarp and some garbage bags. He'd intended on cutting Edie into little bloody bits and letting his uncle dispose of her remains. Stupid greedy bitch!

And that, in a nutshell, was the genesis of their trip to 666.

***

Edie walked out of the bathroom clad in a purple bathrobe.

"Put your clothes back on," Duncan said. "We need to go eat."

She pulled apart the bathrobe, revealing a slim figure with small breasts and wide hips. "First make love to me." She crossed to the bed, lay on it and spread her legs, then cocked a saucy finger at him. "Come on, baby, I won't bite."

Duncan considered telling her to go to hell.

But we are in Hell, he thought, and just like that, he began smiling. All of a sudden, everything seemed funny to him. He could see that Edie was scared behind her sexy front. She'd hidden her terror well, but she was close to freaking out. He was scared too. At the moment he had no idea what they'd do. But sex was something familiar. Sex would relax them both.

"Alright," he agreed, walking towards her.

"Hurry up," she urged as he undressed. "I can't wait."

Her desire for him was so clearly genuine that Duncan felt powerless to refuse her request.

While dropping his underpants to the hotel room floor and letting his swollen penis spring free, Duncan knew his murder quest was about becoming even more complicated. There seemed something very wrong with making love to a woman you intended killing. Or killing one after you'd made love to her.

Then he was naked and in bed with Edie Forrest. He dropped his tongue to her vagina and licked her up and down, while she squirmed beneath him. She was very pent-up. She came immediately. The tension seemed to flood out of her and he felt her relax.

"Enter me now!" she gasped. "Fill me up!"

He slid up the bed and slid into her. She inhaled sharply as he sank into her body and then she began moaning. He began thrusting and once he did so, she seemed to climax almost continually, turning her head from side to side and staring at him with a look of surprise on her face. Duncan found himself wondering at how sexually aroused he was; and at the mystery of sex itself. Now that he was making love with Edie, with her body soft beneath his, he found it impossible to hate her. At the moment, she was the most wonderful woman in the world—the only woman in the world.

"Shit!" he said. "I'm gonna come!"

Hearing this, she reached up and grabbed hold of him. Then she clung on tightly, squeezing her breasts hard against him, while he thrust and groaned and his body tensed up, and on a signal from his testicles, ejaculated. His penis swelled inside her and the sperm squirted out of it. As he came, he kissed Edie savagely, digging his tongue deep into her mouth.

Afterwards, as they lay side by side, she asked him, "That wasn't horrible, was it?"

He shook his head, his right index finger tracing circles around her right nipple. He tried to keep hating her, but couldn't. "No, it wasn't bad at all. You're dynamite."

Visibly pleased with the compliment, Edie rolled off the bed and onto her feet.

"Edie?" he called as she headed for the bathroom door.

"Yeah?"

Duncan pulled himself up and gestured around the motel room. "You're taking this really cool. Aren't you scared?"

Her face seemed to sag. "Baby, I'm scared shitless."

She hurried into the bathroom.

Duncan listened to her shower, thinking: *So, here we are now—two thieves trapped in the middle of nowhere. Shit, Duncan White, if you'd just kept your greedy fingers to yourself. But no, you weren't content with your fat salary, were you? You had to steal Cashstretch's money!*

"Hey, Duncan!" Edie called after a while. "Come on in and shower with me. We need to hurry to the restaurant. I feel ravenous now."

"Yeah," he agreed, getting off the bed. "Let's just hope the food in Hell doesn't taste like shit."

CHAPTER 17

Pearl

In the end, Pearl Harbor ended up not accompanying Slick and Minx to Fat Larry's bar.

Mr. Brooks, who lived upstairs in the Hellton Hotel, had stopped by for a sex session just as they were about leaving.

Mr. Brooks was middle-aged and quite plump. He was short and had blue eyes and cropped brown hair.

Mr. Brooks was obsessed with bondage. Most of his sex sessions with Pearl consisted of him tying her up in various contorted positions. He was an expert with knots, having apparently travelled to Japan for lessons in oriental rope-bondage techniques.

Tonight for instance, Mr. Brooks had Pearl folded double, with her knees up by her shoulders and her ankles lashed behind her head. He'd then bound her wrists to her ankles, and then begun slinging ropes around her torso and breasts too. Tonight's position was an uncomfortable one, but Pearl bore her aches stoically.

One good thing about Mr. Brooks was that he gave very good head. Once he had her tied up to his satisfaction, he always rewarded her for "Being a good girl" by licking her to several orgasms. Now, he began licking her and it was all she could do not to scream out her pleasure.

One reason Pearl tried not to scream was because she could hear the young men in the next room moving about and talking. She didn't want to alarm the new arrivals. Other people moved about outside the room too, shadows against the drawn blinds.

Afterwards, Mr. Brooks, his lips and chin covered with Pearl's juices, sat on the bed and smoked a joint.

"Gimme a drag of that," Pearl said.

"First the test, darling," he said. "Never forget our little bet."

She rolled her eyes, but still tried her best to free herself. He'd promised her a thousand dollars if she could ever free herself from his knots. She'd long ago acknowledged that she'd never win the money. Trying to undo Mr. Brooks' web-work of knots was impossible; a total waste of effort. She was very impressed by how tightly this middle-aged man could tie someone up.

Finally, she quit. "Baby, I ain't Houdini, that's for sure."

Laughing, he held the joint to Pearl's lips and let her take a long pull of the marijuana. "I'm practicing to get better, darling," he said.

"You shouldn't bother," Pearl replied. "You've no competi—"

He'd slipped his erection into her mouth. "Old Chinese saying, darling: Let mouth of slut lick and suck cock, but never talk."

She concentrated on sucking his penis. All in all, sex with Mr. Brooks wasn't too bad a way to spend an evening.

CHAPTER 18

Rick, mostly

Rick and Manny walked back from the Hellton's restaurant.

The pair were eating takeout burgers. They also had a bottle of white wine with them, though the waiter had assured them it tasted like "horse piss."

The burgers tasted okay though. Manny had had a question for the waiter: "What do you call these—Hell Burgers?"

Rick ate slowly. He wanted to mourn his brother Randy, but he knew this was neither the time nor the place. For this auto mechanic from Zanesville, the rules of the game had changed. If the mayor was to be believed, the game now was survival.

At dinner, they'd sat with May and the other newcomers. The Chinese woman hadn't eaten much. She'd drank a beer and explained to them in detail how 666 functioned and what traps to look out for. Everyone had had questions. According to May, here in 666 just about anything could kill you; one had to be alert all the time.

So Rick was working on controlling his emotions. He needed to be sharp as an arrow, alert as a hawk.

It helped that Manny, who seemed to have adapted better to their spatial displacement, kept talking. For his part, Rick ate his hamburger and tried not to brood.

"Man, do you believe what she said—that our arrival here was predetermined by forces beyond our control?" Manny asked as they walked through the empty hotel lobby. While waiting for Rick's reply, he disposed of his burger wrapper in a blue trashcan.

Rick shrugged. "I dunno, man—hurts my head to even consider the implications of her words. "But . . ."

"But what?"

"Well, there is that crazy thing May said . . . about us already having bank accounts here in our names by morning, with five thousand bucks in each." He stared helplessly at Manny. "Dude, you're the sci-fi buff. Make sense of that for me?"

Manny shrugged. "Makes no damn sense. None at all. How did she put it again?"

"She said, here we'll never run out of money. We can earn more by working—either for the town authorities or other people, or by providing some kinda service even, but that there's always gonna be something above minimum wage in our bank accounts."

They'd turned onto the walkway to their room. "You got any job in mind?" Manny asked.

"No-brainer really. I'm a mechanic—I'll check out the used-car lot. You?"

"Nah. I know I definitely don't wanna be a hooker though."

They both laughed at that.

CHAPTER 19

Manny

For his part, Manny Bishop was doing his utmost best to hide his excitement.

I did it! he thought as he and Rick entered their room. *I got us here safely!*

Well, not safely—Randy and Cody were dead, but . . .

Manny shrugged. But nothing. In situations like this one, there was always a price to pay.

Back in their room, he and Rick sat opposite each other; he on the bed, Rick on a chair near the window. Erotic female squeals came through the walls.

Rick put a hand to his bald head and groaned. "I wish those bitches next door would stop fucking for two minutes! They were at it when we got here, and are still going at it now." He flung Manny a pained look. "They keep this up tomorrow and we're gonna move, man."

At that moment the noises died.

"I think they heard you, bro," Manny joked. Then he forgot Rick's complaints, lay back in bed and stared at the ceiling.

***

On a Thursday evening in June two years ago, Manny Bishop had been talking to his girlfriend Michelle on the phone when the line suddenly died. At the time this happened, Michelle Walz had been travelling home from Warsaw, Ohio with her older sister Tessa.

The last things Manny had heard over the dying line were the crackling of static and Michelle yelping: "Oh, my God, where the hell is this? Help, some—!"

That was also the last anyone had ever seen of Michelle Walz. According to Tessa Walz, who'd called home in a panic, on their way back to Zanesville, they'd parked opposite a gas station called the Red Eagle so Michelle could buy a pack of cigarettes. Michelle had crossed the road, entered the convenience store, come out again with her cellphone pressed to her ear, and had been about crossing back to the car when she'd seemingly flickered out of existence.

Tessa later agreed that she might be mistaken as to the details of her sister's vanishing. A white RV had driven out of the gas station, blocking off view of her sister for a second, and even though the camper hadn't stopped—indeed it had picked up speed before passing Michelle—there was the possibility that someone had snatched Michelle. Tessa didn't believe this, but the cops didn't believe the truth either.

The police tracked down the RV. It belonged to Tom Anderson, a famous Boston cop who was on vacation with his girlfriend, Grace Barbanell. Also in the RV were the girlfriend's twin sons Greg and Doug.

Sure, Detective Anderson and Grace Barbanell agreed, they'd noticed a young woman standing by the roadside outside the Red Eagle. She'd been talking on the phone; but so what? Folks made phone calls by the highway all the time. They'd driven past her without a second thought.

Here the trail went cold. Michelle Walz had seemingly vanished into thin air. The police, who were certain she'd been abducted, kept her case file open, but they never got a single lead as to her whereabouts.

About the only person who believed otherwise was her boyfriend Manny. Even though they'd just begun dating, Manny had really loved Michelle. On meeting her, he'd instantly recognized her as his soul mate.

Along with Michelle's family, Manny had been heartbroken over her disappearance. Day after day he'd waited for news that she'd been found; but he really didn't expect her to be. He remembered all too vividly her final words: "Oh, my God, where the hell is this? Help, some—!"

Manny's only interpretation of this was that Michelle had been 'taken' somewhere else. Somewhere weird; somewhere not of this Earth.

After hearing from Tessa Walz the details of exactly what had happened, Manny began his own investigation into Michelle's disappearance, trawling the internet for information. Manny was a sci-fi buff and was already very amenable to the idea of alien abductions. At first that's what he thought had happened: that little green men had zapped Michelle up into orbit.

But then, half a year later, while searching through his call logs in the app he used to save them, Manny noticed that his final phone call to Michelle Walz had occurred at exactly 6 p.m. that evening. His heart had seemed to stop at the ritual significance of his discovery.

Six p.m. on the sixth day of the sixth month of the year? And on Route 666?

After this finding, Manny switched his investigation from alien abductions to supernatural ones. And it was now he discovered that Ohio's Route 666 had a long history of people (and groups of people) going missing, and all of them vanishing on the 6th of June.

And all of them going missing at around 6 o'clock in the evening.

There was no conclusive evidence, of course. But there were several accounts of people—including a six-year-old girl who'd been standing near a car when it 'transitioned'—catching a glimpse of a world where "The sun was reversed and huge 'funny-looking birds' with teeth like Venom's" flew down the highway.

One major investigative glitch was that most people vanished in their cars—so there was literally no evidence left behind.

All this while, Manny's love for Michelle hadn't cooled. Whenever he thought about her, he felt miserable and alone. He desired her smile and her beauty in his life again, brightening his days and making him feel the world was a good place. She'd been the woman he wanted to marry.

Manny's desire and longing for Michelle Walz might have faded if he'd had closure; if the cops had found her corpse. But Manny knew no corpse would ever be found. It wasn't here on Earth to be found.

He knew where his love was and he intended to get her back again.

Of course, Manny hadn't told the others what he intended doing. His close friends were all religious sceptics. They'd have laughed their heads off if he'd suggested he wanted to break into Hell. The only one of the guys who ever went to church was Cody, and that was just twice a year, because Cody's father was a church deacon and insisted on him being in Easter and Christmas services.

So there was no way he could tell them what he planned. But he needed the guys with him. No way could he enter that place alone. Not after everything he'd read online and in the newspaper clippings he'd scanned in the library. The 666-underworld existed, but it was dangerous.

Manny knew there was strength in numbers. Four of them together had more chance of surviving over there than he alone.

So he'd set up the fishing trip for the sixth of June.

If that one didn't work, he'd try to schedule another for next year. Maybe not a fishing trip next time, but a trip to a nightclub out of town. He was committed to entering the under-realm, no matter what.

The idea was to be at the Red Eagle gas station by a few minutes to six p.m. Then he'd somehow force a delay in their departure.

Manny agreed that it might not work, but then again, it just might.

***

It worked. We got here. Sure, Randy and Cody died, but that was the price.

Manny stopped staring at the ceiling; and looked at Rick instead. Of course, if Rick ever suspected that he'd had anything to do with Randy's death . . .

Rick was a hothead . . . and Rick *loved* his younger brother. Rick sat there now with a glass of white wine in his hand. Looking tough-as-nails while trying not to break down in tears. Manny's heart went out to him.

Maybe I should've left the guys out of this, not involved them in this crazy caper. They had no idea what they were getting into. And they didn't wanna bring any guns along on the fishing trip 'cos of Cody's drug-abuse record. Sorry, guys— I didn't intend it to work out like this.

Nice thoughts of course, but pointless if Rick so much as suspected that Manny had intentionally brought them here.

But Manny didn't intend to let that happen. Like everyone else, Rick believed that Michelle had been kidnapped by a serial killer. (The pair had never met either, Michelle being away on campus most of the time.) Manny intended to be very secretive in his inquiries about her possible whereabouts down here, and to pretend enormous surprise on finally locating her. If he could locate her. For all he knew, she might have been killed after her truncated scream for help on the phone.

Baby, please be alive. I've really missed you these last two years. Please be alive! But even if I do find Michelle here, won't she be in love with someone else by now? And then my coming here will all be for nothing. Particularly since everyone— except Ned Shriver—agrees that there's no way to get back to Ohio.

Depressing thoughts.

"How's the wine?" he asked Rick. " 'Horse piss' like the waiter said?"

Rick shook his head. He seemed glad of the opportunity to speak, as if he'd been having depressing thoughts of his own. "Nah, nothing that bad," he replied. "But it's weird all the same. You know how our burgers tasted—not off, but with that weird, almost bitter undertaste as if you're not meant to enjoy them? Same thing with this wine. I guess one'll get used to it."

"Maybe we won't," Manny said. "May said all the food's like that here. Maybe we're not supposed to enjoy the food, or anything else down here."

Rick waved his glass. "*Down* here? Dude, how the hell can we be *underground* if there's a sun overhead?"

Manny got off the bed and strolled past Rick to peel back the window drapes. "Well, first of all, for most religions Hell is supposed to be underground," he said over his shoulder. "Somewhere right in the center of the Earth. And then, in the restaurant, remember May kept referring to us as being 'down here' . . . Ned did that too. Besides, I think the black sun's an illusion. Sure, it's a source of light and heat, but it's too close to us to be a true star. And yet it's also too far away for us to reach; and the mountain walls apparently can't be scaled either. And notice how this sun never moves? Which suggests that it's actually suspended in place, like a light bulb."

"What sci-fi novel or movie did you get that from?"

The door to the next room opened and closed then. A couple strode past Manny's window. The man was short and plump. The woman was slim and busty; she wasn't Michelle. The pair were chatting about what to order in the restaurant.

"The lovers just left," Manny informed Rick.

"Great," Rick said, getting up from his chair and walking over to fall on the bed. "Maybe *now* I'll get some sleep. And I hope that I dream that this is all just a dream and wake up from it in the morning."

"You won't."

"I'm sure as hell gonna try anyway. And if I die before I wake . . ." Then his expression turned puzzled. "Manny, something else is bugging me about this place; something that don't add up."

Manny turned away from the window. "How do you mean?"

"Well, see, earlier on, during our ride into town in Ned's truck, I noticed a church."

"I noticed it too. I wasn't sure, but I saw the crosses. So, what about it?"

"So . . . if this is part of *Hell*, how come there's a *church* here? That's what I was pondering all the time I was sitting in the chair there. What the hell is a church doing in Hell?"

"You know I hadn't thought of that?" Manny agreed, taking up Rick's abandoned place in the chair and filling his own glass with wine. "And it wasn't a satanic church either—the crosses were all right-side-up."

Baffled himself, Manny sipped his wine. Yes, Rick was right, just like their burgers, the wine did taste tainted; enjoyable, but somehow degraded; pleasure that you weren't really meant to enjoy.

"It's a good question," he said solemnly after a while. "What on earth is a *church*—of all buildings—doing down here?"

"Weird name too—Acme Bible Church?"

CHAPTER 20

The Church In Hell

One cold Friday evening last June, Reverend Frank Stevens, pastor of Lancaster's Grace of God Mission, drove his Ford Fiesta into the Red Eagle gas station to fill up. On driving out of the gas station, he'd found himself down in 666.

Reverend Stevens' capture by the Route 666 portal was an oversight, the hell-gate being specifically programmed not to snare preachers.

The problem was, that at the time of his capture, Frank Stevens hadn't exactly been in a state of grace. For one thing, he'd been mad at his wife Helen for accidentally putting his wallet in the washing machine. For another thing, he'd been mad at his board of deacons over their continual attempts to frustrate his expansion of the church's evangelical budget. Last of all, he'd been extremely mad at himself too for accidentally flattening a cottontail rabbit—one of the Good Lord's creatures—that had bounded out in front of his car two miles back.

Reverend Stevens was a preacher of the old 'Fire and Brimstone' mold. His preferred version of God wasn't the modern 'loving father' image, but the old 'consuming fire' version. Sixty-years old at the time, he was tall and gaunt and fearless—accepting no nonsense from any man or devil. His one weakness was his temper, which occasionally got the better of him. Sometimes he even got angry with God, for not pouring out His wrath on sinners fast enough.

The upshot of all this anger was that at that fateful moment on that fateful day, Reverend Stevens had, in the eyes of God, qualified as one of the things he himself despised the most—he'd been a sinner.

Long story short, he'd wound up in 666.

After realizing what had happened, Reverend Stevens had repented of his sins.

And . . . after discovering there was no way out of 666, Reverend Stevens had decided the Almighty had sent him to Hell for a reason and had begun preaching, commanding all and sundry in 666 to repent of their sins.

This of course, was the specific reason why the Route 666 portal rejected *honest* preachers. It didn't matter what religion they professed; they always tried to alter the status quo from darkness to light. If there was one thing that wasn't needed in Hell, it was sermons on the "Efficacy of the blood of Jesus Christ in washing sinners white as snow." It got even worse when this particular preacher founded the Acme Bible Church on the edge of town and drove daily into 666 on preaching forays.

The battle lines between good and evil had been drawn.

At first, there was no real battle to speak of. Without even trying, the demons seem to have won. Everyone in 666 rejected Reverend Stevens' message outright. Had he been more conciliatory and willing to compromise a little, he might have succeeded better in spreading the Gospel, but no one wanted to hear the old man's 'black is black and white is white' message of divine retribution for sin.

Stopping just short of giving him the tar-and-feathers treatment, Father Stevens was run out of town at gunpoint and warned not to return for any reason. Once a week, someone from the sheriff's office drove out to the Acme Bible Church and picked up Reverend Stevens' shopping list, then fetched the items from town for him and drove off again.

Things went on this way for three months.

During that time, the only other person who saw the old preacher was Ned Shriver. On Ned's endless forays back and forth along Route 666 searching for the way out, he'd occasionally stop by the church to see how the old man was faring. Most times he found him in surprisingly good spirits.

Sometimes he'd find Father Stevens praying by the church altar. Ned saw no point in praying down here, but he let it go. Everyone was entitled to their own eccentricities.

It was Ned Shriver who first noticed that the gargoyles never attacked the church.

He'd been driving his armored GMC truck down the highway and a group of about ten of the winged monsters had ambushed him. They were behind him, so he couldn't fire on them, and several had already landed in the pickup truck's rear bed.

Ned knew he'd have a hell of a fight to get out of this alive. On instinct, he'd swerved off the road into the church grounds. The moment he'd passed through the gates, the gargoyles had begun squawking like scared chickens and taken to the air.

Ned had parked his truck, climbed down and stared at the gargoyles. The black monsters all hovered in the air outside the Acme Bible Church premises, making no attempt to come closer.

"This is holy ground," Reverend Stevens said from behind Ned. "They can't tamper with the Lord's consecrated property."

"Holy ground?" Ned asked, as if the idea was a strange one to him.

The old man nodded. "The shadow-things and demons don't come near here either."

"Can you bless and consecrate the town?" Ned had asked.

"Not if you're all gonna keep sinning like bunnies over there," the old man retorted. "God can't be mocked: what a man sows is what he's gonna reap. The wages of sin is death."

Ned nodded. That made sense.

But there was something that Reverend Stevens could and would do. Ned left the church that day armed with several cans of blessed water—holy water. Then he drove back into town and told everyone what he'd discovered.

For three months after that, no one in 666 died from gargoyle attack. All the town residents carried the holy water around with them. All that one required to repel the gargoyles was a plastic bottle with a straw stuck in it. Once you squirted the holy water on the gargoyles, they caught fire and flew off screeching.

Even surprise attacks by the shadow-things reduced in number. The shadow-things could sense the holy water, and once a carrier came close, they'd begin squirming in fear, giving themselves away.

Needless to say, Reverend Stevens' stock instantly went up in town. All of a sudden, he was no longer a pariah. Some of the townsfolk even began attending services at the Acme Bible Church.

Needless to say also, the demons weren't in the least bit pleased by any of this.

***

The demons had a strange relationship with 666. Though hardly ever seen, they made occasional forays in and out of the enclosed space. Most of them seemed to be caretakers. Others had something to do with the river.

Occasionally the demons killed people. Most times though, they just tortured folks who came upon them unawares.

One thing the demons did like was human corpse meat. When someone died, they'd dig up the corpse and carry it off to eat. In the past there had been no way of avoiding this. The town had no crematorium, and the nauseating smell of roasting meat that had accompanied 666's only Indian funeral pyre had convinced everyone that they'd be much better off just letting the demons have the bodies.

But now . . . people were being buried in the ABC church cemetery, with the preacher consecrating both their graves and their corpses. Which of course, meant that the demons no longer had access to the delicious dead flesh.

The demons were infuriated. Something needed to be done about Reverend Stevens and fast at that. But what? The demons didn't dare approach the church.

***

Al Gordon was one of those who'd never liked Reverend Stevens from the offset and who still disliked him even after he'd made 666 safe from the gargoyles.

Reverend Stevens reminded Al of his dead drunk of a father, the man who'd made his life a living hell throughout his childhood years with regular beatings and the assurance that, "You little piece-of-shit; you'll never amount to anything in life!"

The fact that he'd wound up in 666—thus in a sense fulfilling his father's prediction—just made Al that much angrier.

Al's father had been an asshole; he'd told Al he'd be an asshole too; and then he'd gone a step further and turned Al into that asshole he'd predicted he'd become. Now, seeing the preacher just reminded Al of all that and made him mad.

So the demons used Al Gordon to do their dirty work.

Actually, it was Al who sought the demons out. He'd wanted something from them—a magical book from the LOTUS series.

They gave it to him, and in return, as the demoness Hexis sweetly put it after biting off both of Al's ears and eating them, "Consider me Salome, stepdaughter of king Herod Antipas—All I want in return for dancing to your tune is the head of Reverend Frank Stevens on a silver platter."

CHAPTER 21

Crooked Crosses

"And so," May Wong informed her rapt listeners, "Al Gore went over to the Acme Bible Church one evening and beheaded Reverend Stevens. Ned Shriver found the corpse the next day . . . minus its head, of course."

May was still in the Hellton's restaurant. This was an oval room with wide windows to let in the permanent daylight. May had stayed behind after finishing her dinner to answer any questions the newbies had. They had lots of questions.

Five of them sat around a circular plastic table dotted with drinks: herself, the biker and his wife, the old dentist, and a young black stockbroker, the last person to enter the underworld tonight.

The black man was too confused to eat his steak and fries. He just stabbed at the potato strips, never lifting the fork to his mouth. Then he'd drink from his glass of beer, then stab at his fries again while staring at May. May deduced that Ned had been too sleepy to fill this guy in on the details of where he now was.

Somehow, during the questions and answers they'd gotten on to the tale of the underworld's resident psychopath.

"Al took the reverend's head?" the dentist asked.

"Why would he do a thing like that?" the biker lady asked. Her name was Lulu.

"Al's an asshole through and through," May explained. "He didn't just kill the old guy. . . . Afterwards, at the demons' request, he went through his things in the parsonage next door and burnt the preacher's Bible—just in case any of the rest of us had ideas of becoming holy men or women."

She took a sip from her own beer. As usual the beer tasted like it had shit mixed in it, or that slimy goop that filled the river.

"So what happened after that?" the biker asked. The man was thirtyish and very muscular, with long black hair, gray eyes, and an aquiline nose. His name was Dave. May found him handsome despite his heavy beard and mustache. His woman Lulu was his exact opposite: pretty, but small and skinny, with cropped blonde hair and piercing blue eyes beaming from her hawk-like face. May could easily imagine her before a chalkboard, organizing a flock of schoolchildren.

"Everyone was enraged," May replied. "We immediately organized a posse. Every man in town armed himself and they all went looking for Al to lynch him. He wasn't in town, so the men drove down to the Dark Zone to get him. They caught him and roughed him up a little, but while bringing him back to town the gargoyles attacked them en-masse. They say it was like a cloud of them descended over the posse."

"No!" the little biker woman exclaimed, her face taut with fright.

"Fifteen men were killed, torn to shreds by the 'goyles. The rest made it back here alive, but most were wounded. Three later died from their wounds." May sipped some beer and looked around her listeners. "Of course, in the panic, Al got away—the Devil clearly looks after his own. Later, we sent in two more posses, but we never caught Al, who's been living out in the Dark Zone ever since. Assisted by the gargoyles, he makes sporadic raids into town." She looked angry. "Whenever you find a headless corpse around here, you know it's Al Gore's doing."

"What does he want with all the heads?" the black stockbroker asked. The man had introduced himself as Tyrone. May didn't remember the dentist's name.

May's face twisted up with disgust. "Apparently, Al wants to become a demon himself, but to do so he's first got to kill enough people to prove he's ruthless enough. The heads are proof to the demons that he's killed someone."

"What a sicko!" Lulu said.

"So go on," the dentist prompted. "What happened after that?"

May gave a sad smile. "Of course, with the good reverend dead, the church fell into disuse again. We soon ran out of holy water too. Since then—the murder happened six months ago—everything's gone back to the way it used to be, which is how you met us tonight. We stay as alert as possible and somehow survive. It's weird, but you soon get used to living like this. Only thing—"

"Hold on a moment," Dave interrupted. "If holy water's effective against the gargoyles and demons, how 'bout crosses? They should work too, right?"

"Yeah, that's right," the stockbroker agreed. "They come from the same source, represent the same thing, so they should have the same effect. Or don't they?"

May had been prepared for this question. She reached into her purse and produced a pen and a pad. "Here," she told the biker. "Try drawing a cross. Draw a lot of them."

Dave took the pad from her and put pen to paper. A moment later he began looking horrified. "Hey, what is this shit? What the hell am I drawing here?"

May laughed. "What's the matter? You somehow can't control your wrist?"

The biker nodded back in horror, though his girlfriend looked amused. The dentist and stockbroker bent over the table for a closer look. Instead of Christian crosses, Dave was drawing swastikas on the pad.

"What are you, man?" the black man asked. "Some kind of Nazi sympathizer?"

Dave shook his head; he seemed mortified to the depths of his soul.

Lulu laughed. "A Nazi? Him? He's Jewish! Ha ha ha!"

Dave kept staring at what he'd drawn. Lulu tried to control her laughter. May reached across and slid the pad to Tyrone. "Alright, man, your turn. *You* try drawing crosses."

His hand shaking, the black man took the pad from her. He tried drawing, gasped, "I don't believe this shit!" and then held the pad up for the others to view. It was covered with KKK, KKK, KKK. Now Tyrone looked as horrified as the biker.

May retrieved the pad from Tyrone's trembling fingers and offered it to the dentist. "You wanna try drawing crosses?"

He calmly shook his head. "I'm a lapsed Catholic. I'll likely draw someone hanging the Pope."

May gave Lulu an inquiring look. Lulu's mirth instantly drained from her face. She shook her palms at May. "Hell no, I'm already spooked enough as it is."

"Does this *always* happen?" Dave asked, finally getting control of himself.

May put the pad away and nodded. "Always. You can't draw or make crosses here. If you try to make them from wood or steel or even stone, some force warps your creations into something else."

"But the church?"

"Only place here that has any crosses." The Chinese woman finished off her beer. "I've wondered why the demons don't send Al to burn down the place. I think the reason is 'cos he'd have to go in there alone and Ned lives there now—"

Lulu asked, "Ned Shriver? The guy who brought us all here?"

"Yeah, he lives in the church parsonage now. Ned's a loner, so that's alright, I guess. Thing is, Ned's tough too—"

"Amen to that," biker Dave said, lifting a beer can in a salute. "That guy's one tough S.O.B alright!"

May went on: "I think the demons can't risk losing Al in a one-on-one fight with Ned . . . though what the demons need Al so badly for, I've never figured out. Ned ain't in the least bit religious, but the church grounds will protect him and the devils couldn't help Al if Ned got the upper hand." She shrugged. "Anyway, that's my take on why the old church is still standing."

CHAPTER 22

May

Leaving the Hellton at around 1.a.m., May Wong saw Pearl Harbor sitting outside her ground floor room, smoking.

She waved to the prostitute. Pearl either didn't notice her or was too stoned to wave back. May had earlier noticed Pearl entering the restaurant, her arm around Mr. Brooks' waist. Pearl had seemed to be walking in a little pain; as if she had cramps. Mr. Brooks' rope-bondage obsession was known throughout town.

Smiling, May returned her thoughts to her own 'clients' of the evening, all now dispersed to their rooms.

While getting into her car she reflected on the meeting. She felt pleased with the night's work, advising the newbies on their new lives and careers in this terrible place.

This was still night, wasn't it? For an answer, she looked at the nearest town clock, the one across the road on the bank's wall. 1 o'clock in the black half. In theory, one hour past midnight. In practice, the world was as bright as ever.

Feeling suddenly helpless and insignificant, May scowled up at the distant mountain wall. *I hate this place. Oh God, how I want to leave this place!*

She felt sad and disconnected.

Even in this timeless and hellish realm the tyranny of the clock still dominated. At the moment the streets were deserted. Everyone was in bed, waiting for the clocks to strike the 6 at the top, the upper separation between the black and white, so that 'daytime' could resume.

Craziness. Utter insanity.

May Wong was conscientious. She'd been with the welcoming committee for four years now and still remembered her own confusion on arriving here. So she always did her best to help newcomers understand their situation. She had no guarantee of success, however. In the end, adaption and survival depended on each person's mental makeup. Some people—she suspected the white-haired dentist to be one of these—made easy transitions to living below. Others—the biker's wife and the perplexed black stockbroker appeared to fit into this second category—slowly lost their minds and might soon become careless enough to wander off out of town and become food for the gargoyles.

Figuring it couldn't be helped, May Wong drove home.

It was a short drive. She lived down at the other edge of town, up close to the pink haze, which she liked looking at.

It was while opening her front door that May became aware of eyes watching her.

She spun around, dipping into her purse for her revolver. But she wasn't fast enough.

The two gargoyles slammed into her, flinging her back against the house wall. Stunned, May slid down the wall. Before she'd hit the ground, the gargoyles had torn her belly open with their claws and were pulling out her guts and stuffing them into their mouths. Their serpentine eyes glittered with pleasure. Their bear-trap-like teeth first glinted brightly, then reddened with her blood. Their black bat-wings impatiently beat the air. Their long tails lashed about like whips.

May spent the last seconds of her life staring in horror and agony, while her blood spurted out all over the gargoyles; while they slobbered and fought one another for choice bits of her body.

Yes, I wanted to leave this evil place, she thought, *but not like this.*

Once May Wong was dead, the gargoyles ripped her head off. Then, carrying her severed head, and the left arm that stubbornly remained attached to it, the monsters flew off towards the Dark Zone.

CHAPTER 23

Slick, Pearl & Minx . . . Next 'Morning'

Minx walked into the hotel room and flung her handbag on the bed. Next, she sprawled out on the couch. Pearl, who was lying in bed with a joint between her lips, could hear Slick outside, shutting one of their Toyota Camry's doors.

"I went off with Mickey," Minx informed Pearl. "And just like you'd expect, we both got totally wasted."

"How was the sex?" Pearl asked after a long pull on her joint. "Good?"

"Oh, it was swell, girl."

"Yeah? How swollen did he get?"

"Swollen enough!"

Laughing, Minx got up from the couch and went to use the bathroom.

"Wow, what a fun time that was," Slick said, stepping in through the doorway with a bag of groceries. "You should have come with us, Pearl."

"Fat chance of that happening. I was tied up. And you know that once Mr. Brooks ties you up, you're really tied up."

Slick nodded. "So how was *your* last night?"

She shrugged. "I spent a couple of hours trussed up like a poached deer, while he ate my pussy and told me how pretty my ass was. Then he fucked me twice and we went and had dinner. I was so cramped from the position he'd bound me in, I could hardly walk. I still feel stiff." She showed him several rope marks on her left arm.

Slick burst into laughter. "That's one weird fellow, for sure."

"What's funny?" Minx asked, emerging from the bathroom, where she'd had a quick shower, changed into a bathrobe, and was now brushing her red hair. At the moment, Minx looked innocent; she didn't look anything like the whore she was.

Then her face twisted up. "Hey, what's that nasty smell?"

This was classic Minx. She'd act normal and then all of a sudden start acting all extra-sensitive, like a putrid princess.

"What smell are you talking about?" Pearl asked.

"Guys, something *stinks* in here." Minx's voice took on a sing-song quality. "It's making me feel like *puking*."

Pearl rolled her eyes. "Minx, honey, you swallow cum all the time and don't puke. You even eat puke and don't puke. So why all this noise now?"

Minx waved her off. "Slick, baby, please help me have a look?"

"Alright, exactly where are you smelling it?"

Slick began pulling out drawers and looking in them. But Minx had already located the source of the offending odor, right at the bottom of their shared wardrobe.

She leaned back out of the wardrobe and glared at her roommates. "Which of you guys left this fucking hamburger inside my handbag?"

Pearl smirked back at her. "Duh? You did? I think four days ago? It was that night when Joey got drunk and puked on your shoes and you said he . . ."

"Oh yeah, I remember." She peeked in again. "Ugh—and it's got nasty maggots all over it." She stared pleadingly at Slick. "Slick, honey pie, please help me throw this nasty hamburger away?"

Slick paused in undoing his shirt buttons and shook his head. "It's your mess, darling, you throw it away."

Minx's eyes narrowed. "Slick, *please* help me throw this hamburger outside!"

"Hell no."

"Slick!"

Pearl laughed quietly. "Better do like the princess says, man. Her voice is already getting strident. Soon, all the glass in here is gonna start shattering."

"Yeah, yeah, alright. Keep your bloody tampons in." Slick strode over to the wardrobe and picked out Minx's fouled-up handbag, grimacing when he got a good look at its contents. "Wow, you weren't kidding 'bout it being full of grubs. You got any further use for the bag itself?"

"Toss it outside, man. I'll get another one from the shops."

"Sure."

The front door was still open. Slick crossed to it and leaned outside to drop the handbag in the trashcan. Next moment, something black and streamlined hit him from the side.

Slick gave a loud yelp, a noise more of surprise than of pain. The sound startled both Minx and Pearl, who looked up in surprise.

"Hey, man, are you alright?"

But Slick wasn't alright in the least. When he leaned back into the room, his entire left arm, handbag and all, was missing. Slick stood there in the doorway, with blood jetting from his left side and splashing on the door jamb. He had a look of shock on his face and seemed to be trying to get his mind around what had just happened to him. He stared at Pearl and Minx, trying to speak, but seemingly unable to.

The girls were still gaping in horror when black razor-sharp talons pierced through Slick from behind, emerging in red spurts from his chest and belly. Over Slick's right shoulder peeked the ugly head of a gargoyle—all huge tongue and huge teeth and little hungry eyes.

For a few moments, blood dripped from Slick's body like falling rain. Then he was jerked up off his feet and carried out of sight into the air.

Pearl and Minx began screaming.

CHAPTER 24

Rick & Manny

On hearing the screaming coming from next door, Rick and Manny ran outside. They saw the blood all over the entrance to Room 4, looked into the room, saw that both hysterical young women were okay, then finally looked up at the sky.

"Shit! Gargoyles!" Rick said. The sky was dotted with the winged black monsters, several of which carried human burdens.

"We need guns," Manny said. But neither of the two scared prostitutes in Room 4 seemed in any condition to reply any question about weapons that he might ask them; so, along with Rick, Manny watched the sky.

A pickup truck swung into view around the hotel corner then, with Sheriff Hook at the wheel and Mayor Thornwood standing in the back and firing a shotgun up at the gargoyles. Manny followed the angle at which the mayor was aiming her shotgun. One of the gargoyles had a screaming man in its clutches and was climbing higher. One of the mayor's shots must have hit the gargoyle, because a second later, a horrible squawking came from the heavens and the creature dropped its human burden.

The man seemed to explode when he hit the ground. His head cracked open and fell apart in a mess of bone, teeth, blood and brains, and his left arm detached itself completely from his body. The hell-creature must have been eating him while they were airborne too, because his belly was torn open so that his intestines and viscera now scattered redly across the hotel's parking lot.

Sheriff Hook drove his vehicle out of sight. Another pickup truck instantly rolled into view: Ned Shriver, driving with one hand and firing with the other at the black monsters. Sounds of additional shooting came from across the town.

The gargoyles were being beaten back. Within a minute the sky was clear again, with just the exploded corpse in the parking lot as testament to the recent craziness.

That, and the blood Rick and Manny were standing in. Behind them, the two prostitutes had lost their hysterics, but were both still weeping.

CHAPTER 25

Mayor & Sheriff

Rick and Manny were about to try and comfort the girls, when the sheriff and mayor's pickup truck rolled into the hotel parking lot.

Sheriff Hook parked near the dead man. The mayor unlatched herself from the safety belt that had kept her from toppling out of the vehicle while it had been in motion, then leapt down from the truck's rear.

Rick and Manny walked over to have a word, striding past the blue Toyota parked in front of Room 4.

"Hiya there!" the mayor greeted, her long brown hair disarrayed and her large breasts heaving from the effort of the conflict. Then she indicated the mangled corpse. "Hell of a place this is, for sure." She frowned at her sheriff. "Hookie, ain't this the dentist who arrived last night? Please, tell me this ain't him smeared all over the ground everywhere like tomato catsup."

"Yeah, ma'am, I think it's him. He was crossing the road when the 'goyle snatched him."

Mayor Thornwood spat on the ground. "Shit, now I gotta wait again to have my damn toothache fixed. Each time we get a new dentist, they keep gettin' killed—Shit!"

"And Creely's dead too," the sheriff growled in disgust. "First damn deputy I've had in over a year and he gets his dick bitten off by the 'goyles while taking a piss outside."

"Is it always this bad?" Manny ventured to ask.

Sally Thornton peered coolly at him. "Oh, you two are those new guys from last night. How do you mean, 'bad?' "

Rick looked up from studying the dentist's remains. " 'Bad' as in, does this kinda crazy shit happen here every fucking day?"

"Watch your mouth, boy," Sheriff Hook growled, shaking his hook hand out of the truck window at Rick. "This here's the mayor you're talking to, not some trailer-trash tramp." He smirked. "I still ain't forgot you two smartasses from last night's meeting."

"Hey, man, what's your damn problem?" Rick growled back. "I just asked the mayor a question, that's all."

The sheriff scowled at him. "Keep up with that attitude, boy, and one of these days you're gonna give me sufficient justifiable cause to shove this hook of mine up your asshole and jerk your intestines out with it. Just keep flapping that lip of yours, ya hear. I eat jerks like you for breakfast and—"

Mayor Thornwood silenced him with a gesture. "Let it go, Hookie. They're newbies—the cocky attitude'll pass with time. Either that or they'll die."

"Nah, most times, it ain't this bad," she replied Rick with a red lipstick smile. "And we usually never suffer an attack right after we've just gotten in a new batch of people."

"Hey, mayor," Sheriff Hook said, "now that you mention it, *this is* the third attack this week. Has to be a reason for that. That bastard Al Gore's up to something for sure."

The mayor nodded. "Maybe he just needs a few more heads to finish convincing the demons he's worthy of becoming one of 'em," she drawled. "Personally, I wish they'd take the psycho bastard down to the Abyss with 'em and let us have peace of mind up here." She studied the dentist's remains again, then, looking between Rick and Manny, noticed the blood splattered over the entrance to Room 4. "Hey, what happened over there? They lose anyone?"

"We think the gargoyles got the guy who lives in there," Manny explained. The girls are still in shock, so we aren't sure yet."

The mayor's face turned angry. "Shit! Slick's gone? Who the hell are we gonna get to replace him, before all the widows start raisin' hell again?"

Then, her huge breasts straining as if they'd burst her sweat-stained blue shirt, she regarded Manny with an appraising eye.

"Hey, Hookie, is this kid good-looking or what? I think he'll make a great sex worker, don't you? The ladies'll just flip over him."

The sheriff stroked his goatee, looked Manny over, then began laughing. "I dunno, ma'am. But it'll keep him . . . nah, keep both of 'em outa trouble, for sure."

Manny gaped at Mayor Thornwood. "Se-se-sex workers? You want us to be prostitutes? Male hookers?"

"Forget it," Rick said flatly. "Ain't ever gonna happen."

Sheriff Hook's voice now became conciliatory. "Now, don't take it like that, boys. Down here, prostitution's a respectable calling. Lots of single women—for instance, all those who lost their men in today's shenanigans . . . and the pay's really good." When Rick still looked adamant, the sheriff nodded. "Yeah, I know it's a shock, but talk to those two girls in there, they'll give you the full lowdown. Then you can decide, right?"

"Alright," Manny said hesitantly. "We'll think on it."

The mayor and sheriff both nodded. Mayor Thornwood walked round the vehicle, got in and leaned over Hook to blow Rick and Manny a kiss. "So, there you have it, boys: consider what the good sheriff just told ya. You both talk to Pearl and Minx and then come see me in the office tomorrow and tell me your decisions."

Then she brightly chirped: "Like I always say: whoredom's the best cure for boredom!"

"Don't you worry about the mess," the sheriff added before driving off. "Cleanup crew'll be around in a bit to scrape the dentist off of the concrete."

Then they drove off, leaving the two young men dumbfounded.

"Can you believe that shit?" Manny asked Rick. "*Us* as sex workers?"

"I'd rather cut my dick off than stoop that low," Rick said. "That sheriff guy is a total jerk."

Manny nodded. "Yeah." He slapped Rick on the back. "Come on, man, let's go check on how the girls are doing after their fright."

They turned their backs on the exploded corpse and headed for Room 4.

CHAPTER 26

Duncan & Edie

When the shooting began, Duncan was making love to Edie. At the gunshot noises, he made to get off her, but she held him firm so he couldn't get away.

"It could be just about anything happening out there," she sighed at him. "So, let's finish what we've started first before having a look." To emphasize her point, she dug her fingernails into his buttocks.

With his orgasm fast approaching, Duncan wasn't about to argue with that. So they ignored the gunshots and screaming outside. Spreading Edie's thighs wide, Duncan tried to get every available inch of his penis into her, to be as deep inside her as he possibly could. She seemed to appreciate his efforts, squirming and moaning delightedly beneath him. Then the dam burst and he poured out into her.

"We don't have any condoms," he said afterwards. "You'll get pregnant if we keep on like this."

"I won't, I've got one of those contraceptive implants. It's good for another year at least."

"How about disease? You could catch something from me."

She leaned up on her elbow, stroked his hairy chest, and laughed. "And you could catch something from me too. Don't be silly, Duncan, let's just enjoy ourselves."

He leaned over and kissed her. "It's hard, you know?"

"What is, your cock? At the moment, it looks soft and tired."

"It's hard to enjoy myself knowing where we are now."

Edie laughed and got out of bed. She walked over to the window and looked out. "At least the damn gunshot noises have stopped. I can't see over the balcony from here, but I hear people talking downstairs. Can't hear what they're saying though."

"So maybe you're right and it was nothing after all?"

She nodded without turning around. "Maybe. No, I don't think so. There's some activity across the street; a crowd's gathering."

"Oh, we'll check it out later," Duncan said. "You have a great ass. You know that?"

Now she turned, pretty and sexy with her long blonde hair and great body. "And I thought you didn't like me." She squeezed her chest at him. "Admit it, my boobs aren't bad either."

"They're fantastic," he agreed. "I just feel bad, us doing this to my girlfriend?"

Edie rolled her eyes. "You might as well stop feeling guilty about that. Cheryl's literally a world away now." Her eyes misted. "Here, baby, it's just you and me."

Duncan nodded. "Yeah, it is." He reached out a hand to her. "Hey, don't cry. Come back to bed. Now *I am* hard again."

"Are you trying to wear me out?" she teased as she climbed on him and guided his throbbing manhood back between her legs. "You won't succeed, you know. I've been planning what I'll do to you for ages."

"So have I," he said. "So have I, baby."

This time, after they were done, Edie went to use the bathroom.

"You want some orange juice?" Duncan called from the front room.

"Yes please, darling. Then I'd like to walk around and see what this crazy place is like in the daytime."

He could hear her peeing in there. "No difference. It's always daytime here." The statement made him look at the two-toned clock on the wall, opposite the foot of the bed. The time was 9 a.m.—'in the white,' as they said here.

"Oh, you know what I mean," Edie was explaining. "I want to see how this place looks with people everywhere. I also want us to visit the bank across the road. Remember we're supposed to collect our checkbooks and bank ID today. Though I really don't understand how they can be ready when we never applied for them, and how this place has a banking system at all . . ."

While she talked, Duncan got up and padded quickly over to the closet and opened his attaché case, which was stashed in the closet bottom. He felt inside the pocket in the case's cover, palmed the vial of colorless liquid he found there, then shut the case again.

The orange juice, purchased at the gas station last night, was still in the plastic shopping bag. Duncan got it out, filled a glass for Edie and one for himself, then, standing so his back was to the bathroom door and would block her view of what he was doing if she emerged from there unannounced, he laced Edie's orange juice with the knockout drops in the vial. Then he hid the vial between the couch cushions.

The stuff had no taste. It would put Edie to sleep for at least two hours.

More than enough time for him to kill her.

"Hey, your orange juice is ready! You coming out of there to drink it, or do you want me to serve you on the toilet? In fact, a better question is—are you *ever* coming out of there?"

"Ha ha, funny guy. I'll be out in a sec."

When she reemerged, he watched her drink the spiked juice and smack her lips. "Great. Just what I needed after sex. That stuff they serve here? Ugh, even the water . . ."

Then she sighed and yawned. "Dammit, Duncan, I had no idea you could screw like that. You've worn me out completely." She yawned again, wider this time, so much so that Duncan imagined he could stick his hand inside her mouth and bloodily yank her blackmailing tongue from her throat.

Edie felt her forehead with the back of her hand as if testing her temperature, then yawned again. "Darling, I need to lie down."

He caught her as she slumped and carried her across to the bed. The remaining third of her orange juice had spilled over the couch.

He laid her down gently on the bed. Her eyes were shut, but as he was backing away from her, she opened them once, stared dreamily up into his eyes, and softly droned, "Now, you naughty, naughty man, don't you dare take advantage of me while I'm asleep. No screwing me while I'm out cold. That's rape, you know."

"I wouldn't dream of it," Duncan said sweetly.

Her eyes shut and her head lolled on the pillow. She had a smile of pleasure on her face; looked like a painted saint.

Duncan waited till she'd begun breathing evenly, then he walked over to the closet again and got the razor-sharp Walmart hunting knife out of his suitcase.

CHAPTER 27

Rick & Manny, Pearl & Minx

Inside Room 4, the two girls had recovered somewhat. Pearl was shivering though. Minx was gaping wide-eyed at the two young men who'd just walked through the door; she had just sufficient presence of mind to tighten her bathrobe around her. Similarly, Pearl's nightgown had ridden up to her thighs, exposing her long legs.

"Hi! I'm Manny and this is Rick."

"Shit, man," Minx moaned, "the 'goyle just snapped Slick up, snapped him up . . . as if . . . as if . . ."

"Calm down," Manny told her. "Damn, this whole place is so fucked-up."

"Yeah," Rick agreed from behind him. "Someone's gonna have to clean up this mess on the door, or you girls are gonna need a new room."

Manny, meanwhile, had now gotten a good look at the pretty young redhead addressing them. His eyes widened in disbelief. "Michelle? Michelle?"

"Who's Michelle?" Rick and Minx both asked.

Manny, still beside himself with shocked delight, turned to Rick. "Michelle Walz! You know, man—my girlfriend who went missing two years ago!" He spun back towards Minx and jabbed a finger at her. "It's her! It's really her! It's Michelle!"

Rick stepped up beside Manny and looked Minx over. "Dude, I never met her, so I gotta take your word for it."

"I showed you guys her pictures on my phone."

Rick nodded. "Yeah, true, but that was ages ago. I've forgotten what she looked like. But . . . but if this is her, why the hell is she looking like she's never seen you before?"

Which was true. Minx *was* staring at Manny with confusion on her face. "Who-who-who are you?"

He walked over and took her in his arms. "I'm your boyfriend Manny!"

She pulled back a little and looked up at him. *"Boyfriend? Manny?"* Behind her perplexed green gaze and furrowed brow, her mind was clearly hard at work trying to make sense of what this handsome stranger was saying.

"Yes," Manny said. "I'm Manny Bishop, your boyfriend. We were gonna get married and then you went missing."

Minx turned to Rick. "Is he serious?"

Rick nodded. "Yeah. You vanished one evening while on a trip with your sister. Everyone assumed a serial killer got you."

Minx looked back at Manny, shaking her head as if defeated. "Sorry, man. I'm trying really hard here, but I just don't remember you."

Manny looked at Pearl in confusion. "She doesn't remember me—she doesn't remember me. What the hell is wrong with her?"

Pearl sighed. "Man, it's a loooooonng story. You're gonna hate it." She gestured to chairs. "Have a seat, guys. And, Manny, you're right—her real name *is* Michelle Walz. Well, at least it was until that bastard Al Gore kidnapped her."

"Kidnapped?" Manny whispered. "Aw shit!"

***

"So that's what happened," Pearl concluded ten minutes later. "Ned Shriver found her bleeding in the middle of the road. Once she got back from the clinic, she picked up from where she'd left off, but her yesterdays were a total blank, her mind wiped clean. I know she had a boyfriend—she might have even shown me some snaps of you, but that was over a year ago."

Manny stared over at Michelle or 'Minx Fortune,' as she now called herself. This reunion wasn't going anything like he'd imagined it would. Total amnesia? The young woman beside him seemed to almost be someone else; someone alien to him. And if she seemed that way to him, who *remembered* her; how must he seem to her, who'd completely forgotten him?

Well, at least I've found her. That's a start. And best of all, Rick doesn't suspect that I set this whole thing up.

This last fact was great. In that sense, things had worked out much better than Manny could ever have scripted them. He'd been so genuinely shocked to discover Michelle so fast (and living right next door to them at that), that he'd not needed to feign his surprise.

He looked sideways at Minx (he'd decided to stick to the name she was familiar with) and smiled at her. "It's marvelous to see you again, darling, even if you don't remember me. I'm sorry you had to go through all that shit 'cos I wasn't here to protect you."

"You know, baby," Minx said, standing up, "I am starting to remember you now. It's real hazy though, like someone's opening a door in my head into a room that's packed full of fog . . . but I keep seeing your face, and we had some happy times together for sure up on Earth. I'm even seeing you pegging me in bed like you're setting up a tent or something."

"Keep trying, girl," Pearl said encouragingly. "It'll come back to you."

Minx shook her head. "Nah, the effort of recollecting is giving me a headache. Everything's so blurred and hazy." Then she pulled Manny up beside her. "Know what I'd like to do now, baby? How 'bout if me and you go over into your room and make ourselves comfortable there, and then you can tell me everything I need to know about myself. How's that sound to you?"

Manny nodded. "Sounds great. You've no idea how much I've got to fill you in on."

***

"She's off to fuck him," Pearl said after they'd left. "I dunno, his dick might do her good—maybe she's hidden her memories in her pussy. With that bitch you never can tell."

Rick laughed.

"He's acting like he's won the lottery," Pearl added. "She's a total bitch and he's besotted with her. I should be so lucky."

"He's in love," Rick excused. "Dude almost had a nervous breakdown after she went missing. I'm happy he's found her again."

"He'll puke once he discovers some of the things his girlfriend is into now."

"Maybe, maybe not. I say we let 'em work it out."

Rick stretched in his chair and stared out of the open door. The cleanup crew had just arrived, wearing their yellow plastic suits. Almost like a Hazmat team back home. One of them was reeling a coil of intestine into a plastic bag.

Rick looked back inside, running his eyes over Pearl's body; her toned, exquisite form barely concealed by her sheer nightie. Her full breasts in particular magnetized him, the way her nipples pressed temptingly against the transparent pink fabric.

"So what now?" he asked. "What are *we* gonna do while they're both . . . ?"

Pearl lit up a joint. "Except for the fact that it's Slick who got killed today, this is just a typical day in the underworld. Deal with it, man. We're all fucked, so we fuck to forget that we're fucked. Understand?"

She got up and walked past Rick, handing him the joint as she went by.

"Poor Slick," she said as she closed the front door. "He was a darling friend. And yet he's not gonna have a funeral." She wiped a tear from her left eye. "All we can do is screw to mark his passing." She crossed back to Rick. "How does some sex sound to you? Down here it's the best way to relieve tension; that's one reason us hookers are so much in demand. So, how 'bout it? You guys haven't been to the bank yet, have you?"

Rick gulped and shook his head. "We were gonna go, when—"

She slipped out of her nightgown, revealing everything to him, all of herself; nude and gorgeous. "Don't worry, Ricky, this one's on the house. If I don't release some tension myself, I'm gonna go crazy and kill myself."

She knelt before him, helped him slip down his pants and took his turgid penis into her mouth. Rick began gasping at the expert play of her tongue over his penis.

Beside them in an ashtray, the ignored joint filled the air with reefer smell.

CHAPTER 28

Minx & Manny

Next door, Minx was getting undressed too.

"But you don't remember me!" Manny protested as she undid her bathrobe.

"We can work on that later," she said, letting the bathrobe slip to the floor, then running her fingers through her crimson hair and fanning it out over her shoulders. "I'm horny and you . . . well, you've been masturbating to your sad memories of me for two years now, haven't you?"

"Em, not exactly. That would be too morbid."

"Anyway," she went on, "what I'm getting at is, except in my mind, we're not exactly strangers to one another. I get flashes in my brain now of you coming so hard in my pussy, it's like you're impregnating me with six babies at once. So, if we do it right away, we're just like, picking up where we left off?" She pouted. "C'mon, darling—show me how much you've missed me."

Manny couldn't fault her argument. He'd dreamed of this moment for two long miserable years; imagined their passionate reunion in glossy detail. He stripped off fast and got to work licking her clitoris.

Her vagina tasted even better than he remembered. As he swirled his tongue around inside her body, with her gasps and moans raining on him non-stop, he was glad he'd found a way down here to 666 to be with his beloved again.

"Yeah, Manny," Minx gushed as she began to come, "you really must've been my boyfriend in that previous life—your tongue knows exactly what my pussy likes!"

CHAPTER 29

Pearl & Rick

"So, why do they call you Pearl Harbor?" Rick asked when they were done.

Pearl giggled. "Can't you tell, man? It's 'cos I'm a kamikaze fuck and a delight to dock your dick in."

"Oh yeah. I can dig that." He stroked her left thigh. "You sure ain't playing games in bed."

She nodded towards the wall between the rooms. "Minx is even more kamikaze fun than I am. She fucks like she's making war, not love. Not any more though, I guess . . . not now that her boyfriend's turned up. She looks to be on her way to becoming a honest woman again. A retired slut."

"Don't be too certain of that."

"No? Why not?"

Rick's face twisted up. "The mayor and the sheriff are trying to convince Manny and I to join you girls as sex workers."

"Oh." Pearl began laughing like mad. "That'll be nice," she said on calming down. Then on seeing his face: "You don't want to? It's not like back on Earth. Here, it's mostly fun and no one judges you at all."

Rick waved his hands in the air. "Baby, I'm a mechanic. I like getting my hands dirty and greasy in an engine."

Pearl sat up and shrugged. "Yeah? So . . . who says you won't get your hands dirty and greasy as a prostitute? The only difference is the type of engine: soft female flesh instead of hard steel. And the lube cleans off a whole lot easier too."

He shook his head stubbornly. "Babe, it ain't the same."

She laughed. "I never said it was. Fucking is more fun than working."

"Not when fucking *is* working."

She laughed even louder. "Trust me, Ricky darling, after a while you won't be able to tell the difference."

CHAPTER 30

Duncan

"Oh, shit, I can't kill her!" Duncan groaned aloud. "I don't believe it—I can't kill this evil scheming bitch!"

Edie was still out cold from the drugged orange juice. She still lay in bed, but her slumbering form was now stretched out on blue tarpaulin so that her bloody death wouldn't mess up the sheets. Duncan, now dressed in shorts and a tee shirt, was sitting on the bed beside her, hunting knife in hand.

He'd been trying to either stab Edie or slit her throat for thirty minutes now. He could visualize her murder clearly in his mind, could see the moment when he sank the gleaming knife into her creamy skin and her parting flesh wept tears of blood, but . . . he found he couldn't go through with it.

Once, he'd held the blade poised at Edie's throat for five agonizing minutes. All he'd had to do was move his hand slightly and the resulting slit jugular vein would quickly exsanguinate her, but he'd been unable to make the cut.

After a while, Duncan got up. It looked like he wouldn't be killing Edie Forrest after all.

After retrieving the tarp from under Edie's body and packing it and the hunting knife away again, he got dressed. While dressing, he considered this new twist in the tale:

I guess it's best that I don't murder her. We're both stuck here and if we're to make the best of things we're going to need each other.

Smiling now, Duncan walked over to the bed and bending, kissed Edie gently on the lips. He was surprised at how tender and protective towards her he now felt. When his lips touched hers, she smiled and murmured contentedly in her slumber.

Then Duncan left the room to have a walk around town. No point waiting for Edie to wake up. She was certain to be asleep for a while yet.

CHAPTER 31

Minx & Manny, Pearl & Rick

"So, more or less, that's how the store system works here," Pearl explained as they left the drugstore. "You pay for what you want and they give it to you. Just like back home."

"This is crazy," Rick said. "You just bought a quarter-kilo of marijuana over the counter. If that crazy one-handed sheriff catches us now . . . shit!"

"Relax, man," Pearl said, slipping her arm through his. "Hookie smokes more weed than we do."

"The mayor prefers cock though," Minx said. "Sorry, I mean coke . . . you know, cocaine, not Coca Cola. She likes cock too though, but she also powders her nose from time to time."

"So both the mayor and the sheriff of 666 do drugs." They were standing by the curb, waiting to cross the road. Manny jerked a finger back at the drugstore entrance. "I saw jars of white powder on the shelves behind the old storekeeper. Was that . . . ?"

"Cocaine? Yeah, sure. This is Hell, after all."

Minx added: "Guys, lighten up. In Hell you'd expect a drugstore to sell . . . you know, *drugs*—narcotics? . . . They've got speed in there too, bennies, uppers and downers, H, X, peyote, you name it . . . crack even. You can buy it legally here."

"But where does it all come from?" Rick asked, genuinely confused now. "Who supplies everything down here?"

"That's the question no one can answer." Minx dipped her fingers into Manny's shirt pocket and pulled out his brand new Bank 666 ID card, which had his picture printed on it. "It's as unsolvable a mystery as this other one—who puts the money in our bank accounts? Who registers us here in this insane place?"

Pearl nodded. "Guys, you saw it for yourselves. Your accounts were ready when you walked into the bank. You didn't need to pose for any photos—your picture was already on your ID."

"And you spend American money here?" Manny asked.

"Yeah we do, darling," Minx replied. "Genuine dollars straight from the US mint. That's been tested and confirmed too, by comparing our currency notes here with those you newcomers bring with you. Nothing's counterfeit about our money. Even the Treasury Secretary's signature is the same."

Rick shook his head. "This is just unbelievable."

Pearl laughed. "Relax, you'll get used to it."

"Yeah, we're right at home in this place," Minx said. "Except of course, for the lack of the internet and electricity and telecoms."

"And the damn 'goyles everywhere," Pearl added.

Minx nodded. "Yeah, those hungry fuckers too."

They crossed the road, then walked downtown (towards the pink end of the highway) and sat on a bench facing a diner.

***

It was mid-afternoon. The streets were mostly deserted; the townsfolk not yet recovered from the morning's gargoyle attack.

Most of Rick and Manny's day up to this point had been spent this way, loitering up and down town, with the girls pointing out the sights to them, and explaining how things worked around here. Seeing as Minx was with Manny, Pearl had naturally paired up with Rick.

To Manny's delight, a large portion of Minx's memory seemed to have returned. She'd been clinging tightly to him all day, kissing and hugging him. He'd never felt so happy in his life.

But, wow, the power of a bad experience. In bed, 'Minx' was nothing like the 'Michelle' Manny had previously known. They'd made love three times before Minx was satisfied, and each time she came the look in her green eyes was one of intense hatred for him. Manny wished he could get a hold of Al Gore and wring the bastard's neck for messing up Minx's brain like this. The scars all over her body bore witness to how much he'd abused her.

But, on a positive note, she remembered him now, or at least remembered enough about him to be glad to have him back. They were almost like young lovers again.

***

"There's four or five sex stores in town—lots of porn mags, but it's mostly extreme stuff, like scat, violent BDSM, torture, bestiality and some snuff too. The sort of stuff guaranteed to wipe the smile off of God's face."

"The sex shops even stock kiddie-porn. Sheriff turns a blind eye to that 'cos there's no kids here for pervs to molest. Besides, it's a waste of time removing it from the shelves anyway. Do so and a fresh selection of kiddie-porn mags will be back on display by morning."

"Ha ha ha! Pearl and I get lots of requests to dress up as schoolgirls though."

"No kids? A pregnant woman arrived with us yesterday."

"Pregnant? Well, not for long."

"Yeah, she'll soon miscarry. Something in the water or the air here does that to you. I think it's how we never catch STDs either."

After making this last comment, Pearl looked puzzled. "That's always struck me as odd, you know. I'd assume they—whoever runs this place—would *want* us to be sick."

Minx scowled. "Pearl, I told you—if we're sick, no one'll want to fuck us. No one'll be sinning all the time and pissing God off—so the system's set up so we don't fall sick!"

"And I've told you over and over, girl, that I don't believe we were abducted just to sin. I never agreed with Reverend Stevens' POV that this is purgatory either, but . . . Minx, I don't get why you're so into this 'angering God' trip of yours. We're here just 'cos we're here, and we're making the best of it." She glanced up towards the black sun and shuddered. "Personally, I've sufficient trouble just being in this place without actively seeking more from on high."

"Oh, you're just a wimp," Minx said with a cold smirk. Then she noticed that Rick's gaze was fixed on the diner opposite. "Man, what's with you?"

"Yeah, dude," Manny added after giving Minx a kiss. "We can go in there for coffees if you like." He shook the bank card. "We got money now, bro!"

"Nah, I ain't hungry. I'm just trying to work out who refills everything. Even the gas pumps at the stations."

"Wow," Pearl said, staring seriously at Rick. "Well, I think it's time we give you the standard warning around here."

"Warning? 'Bout what?"

"Well, it's like this: wonder all you like about whatever you like, but don't—and I can't emphasize this enough, man—don't you dare take *any* practical steps to find out for sure."

Rick looked questioningly at Minx, who nodded back. "She's telling you the truth. That's how stuff works around here."

"But why?" Manny asked, now as puzzled as Rick.

"Because the powers that run 666 don't like us snooping and prying," Pearl explained.

"You better lay it out for them in more detail," Minx told her.

Pearl nodded. "Yeah, I'd better. Alright, guys, a few years ago, shortly after I got here, a few guys decided to try and find out who was restocking the stores at night." She sighed. "In theory, all they had to do to do this was stay overnight in say, a supermarket or one of 666's many liquor stores, right?"

Both young men nodded. "Right."

"The problem with that," Minx said, "is that there's clear signs on the walls of each shop in town, stating that the premises *must* be vacated by its employees by 2 p.m. at the latest."

"Yeah?" Rick asked.

Pearl nodded. "Every shop here has several such signs in it— Vacate by 2 p.m. And as far as I know, up till then no one had ever tried to do otherwise. But on that fateful night, ten volunteers did defy the golden rule, keeping watch in different stores across town to see who was restocking the shelves with goods."

"What did they find out?"

"Nothing. The lesson was for the rest of us. The next morning there were ten new widows in town. We held a mass funeral."

"Shit!" Manny said, looking scared.

Pearl nodded. "Yeah, man, we had ten frigging corpses—all the investigators had been killed. Their funerals were conducted together 'cos there was a lot of doubt as to who was who. All the bodies had been butchered beyond recognition, their heads and limbs torn off and lots of their flesh eaten." She looked sick as she recounted the memory. "Shit—there was blood all over the shops' walls and bits of intestine piled like stock on their shelves, as if whatever had killed the men had played games with their remains afterwards. Those remains—whatever the sheriff and his deputy could scrape off the walls, ceilings and floors—were all shut inside a single wooden casket and buried like that. That all ten men's remains fit into one casket should tell you how little of them there was left."

"Fuck," Rick said.

Pearl gave a cold laugh. "Like I said, Ricky, it was a huge lesson to everyone else here to abide by the rules. And also a very sobering reminder to us that we were in Hell."

Minx laughed. "Of course, since then no one else has tried to unravel 666's dirty secrets. Everyone now accepts that this place runs on its own infernal rules. All we gotta do is play by those rules and hope nothing else kills us."

"And here, there's a whole lot of bad things that can kill us," Pearl finished. "So, Ricky baby, there's the heads up. Keep to it and you might keep your head."

"Don't worry 'bout that," Rick assured her. "You've convinced me." He stared at Manny. "Come on, man, let's have the girls take us over to the used-car lot, so we can pick out a ride to replace the one we lost last night. I also wanna see if they can use a mechanic."

CHAPTER 32

The Airborne Prostitute

They'd hardly taken ten steps towards the used-car lot when it happened:

Something huge and black and fluid and with a lot of teeth swooped down over the roof of the bungalow on their right and headed for them.

Everyone tried to get out of the way. Three of them made it. Manny shoved Minx off to one side, but the solitary gargoyle switched direction, grabbed her and flew off with her.

Manny leapt to his feet and watched it soar away, its massive black batwings beating the air, Minx dangling below it like a toy. She was screaming for help, but the monster didn't appear hungry yet; it wasn't tearing at her.

"NO!" Manny howled and began pacing nervously. "NO NO NO!"

Down the road, a man walking his German shepherd pulled the dog out of harm's way into a liquor store entrance.

Rick and Pearl got to their feet and stared at the sky too. Flying parallel to the highway out of town, the gargoyle was shrinking fast, becoming a black dot against the gray heavens.

"Where the hell is it taking her to?" Rick asked.

"Where else, baby?" Pearl replied. "To the Dark Zone, of course. Looks like Al Gore has some unfinished business with her."

"No!" Manny said, tears in his eyes. "I just found her again, and this happens?"

Pearl shook her head at the airborne dot as its distance from the town increased. "Hot damn. Minx got abducted *again?* She should change her name to *Jinx.* Talk about bad luck."

"We gotta rescue her," Manny said miserably.

"Forget it," Pearl told him. "It can't be done. Lightning doesn't ever strike twice in the same place. She may have gotten away once, but this time that girl's gone for good."

"No, she's *not* gone for good!" Manny yelled at Pearl in a rage of passion. "I came here—to this horrible subterranean world—to find Michelle! I risked my goddamn life to get here! Now I've found her and I'm sure as hell not letting her go just 'cos some overgrown flying lizard abducted her!'"

"Alright, so you love her," Pearl agreed. "Hey, man—let go of me, you're hurting my arms!"

"Huh?" Manny hadn't even been aware that he'd been shaking her. He let go of Pearl. "Sorry."

"We'd better hurry if we wanna catch it," Rick said quietly, his eyes focused on the sky. "The sooner we get a move on, the more likely we'll find her unhurt."

"You're going out there with him?" Pearl asked Rick. "Man, no one comes back from the Dark Zone. It's just corpses and bones out there. And Al Gore, of course."

Rick kissed her. "Don't worry, babe. I'll be back."

"Why's this so important to you?" she asked.

Rick shrugged. "We can't keep losing people, can we? Yesterday I lost my brother; today Manny's losing his girlfriend? I'm not trying to play hero here, but the shit's gotta stop somewhere."

"It does," Pearl said. "This whole fucking realm is a toilet."

"Rick, we gotta hurry, man!" Manny said. In the sky, Minx and the gargoyle that had abducted her were no longer visible.

"We need a ride," Rick said. "We'd better hurry down to the car lot and—"

"Take ours," Pearl offered quickly. "It's the blue Camry parked in front of our hotel room. There's gas in the tank and the key's in the ignition."

"Thanks," Manny said as they set off running back towards the hotel. "Have you girls got any guns in your room?"

"Yeah," Rick seconded. "We need to be armed and dangerous when we arrive there."

"Slick has—had . . . shit, he's dead!—he had a shotgun, and I've a revolver. Minx didn't like guns, she said they made her nervous."

"We'll take 'em both. Hey, d'you have any idea *where* in the Dark Zone Al Gore lives?"

Pearl searched her mind while she stood panting on the first-floor walkway. "I'm not exactly sure, but it's supposedly on the left as you drive in there. It's a white two-story building. Al calls it the 'White House'—a sick joke, of course."

***

Five minutes later, Rick and Manny were speeding out of town, burning rubber along Route 666. Rick was at the wheel of the blue car.

"I hope Michelle's fine," Manny said miserably. "I don't know what I'll do if that damn 'goyle hurts her."

"Don't worry," Rick said. "We'll rescue her; we'll get her back. Thank heavens it's only a short drive. We just need to find Al's—OH SHHIIIIITT!"

Alarm written all over his face, Rick swerved the blue Camry to the side of the road.

He parked the car and hunched over the wheel, breathing hard. "We hit something! We hit something! Some fucking hell-creature that ran out into the road!"

Manny had been staring at Rick, not at the road. He hadn't seen what they'd struck. He sat there shivering. "We need to hurry," he said finally. "Michelle's life is ticking away with each second we waste!"

"We can't drive on with that thing hanging onto the car," Rick insisted. He looked really nervous. "If it's the same kind of thing that got Randy, we're screwed."

"What did it look like?"

"Like the other one last night—black and tentacled. It must have been laying out here on the highway till we came along and then . . ." He shook his head. "Look, man, let's just get out and have a look for it. Shouldn't take us too long." He pointed down the highway to where the coiling black sky dominated. "We're halfway to the Dark Zone now—we can spare a minute. We don't wanna be arriving in the Dark Zone with something like this tagging along for the ride."

"Alright," Manny nervously agreed. "Guns?"

Rick picked up the shotgun lying by the gearshift. "Pistol's yours, dude. Just don't shoot me in a panic."

Moving with extreme caution, they both got down. They saw nothing either beside or behind the car.

"Cover me," Rick said. "I'll have a look under the car."

Manny stood guard, staring from mountain wall to mountain wall, while Rick got down on his knees and peered beneath the Toyota Camry. They'd parked fifty yards before one of the turnoffs that led to a bridge over the stinky Muskingum River and thence to the mile-distant mountains.

This place is like being locked in a big room with no way out, Manny thought.

"You see anything down there?" he called down to Rick.

"I think so." Rick straightened up. "You have a look—in front, wrapped around the axle. Looks like a melted tire."

"Ugh," Manny said, but in a hurry to get moving, he got down on his knees and also peered under the vehicle. "Nah, man, you're wrong. I don't see anything down here."

"That's 'cos there ain't anything to see down there, asshole," Rick explained as Manny began getting up.

Then he knocked Manny out cold with the butt of the shotgun.

CHAPTER 33

Payback's A Hitch . . .

When Manny revived, he discovered that Rick had stripped him naked and bound his hands and feet with strips torn from his denim pants. His hands were tied behind his back.

He and Rick were still where they'd stopped, near the river bridge turnoff, and he was lying out in the highway, behind the car.

"Hey, c'mon, man," he protested. "What is this?"

Rick smiled like a shark. "See, I just realized that you set all this up—our trip to this hell on Earth. You wanted to come here and find Michelle, right? And so you conned me and my brother and Cody to go with you on that damn fishing trip, didn't you?"

Manny's eyes widened with fright. "No, no, Rick, we're totally here by accident. I'm serious, I had no idea that Michelle was here, bro. You gotta believe me!"

Rick laughed. "That ain't what you told Pearl Harbor a short while ago. You told the girl that you risked your life to get here." He laughed louder as Manny's eyes widened even more. "Yah, I heard you, I just acted like I didn't. And if you risked *your* life to come here, it stands to reason that you risked *our* lives too: mine and Cody's and . . ."—now tears filled Rick's eyes—"and my kid brother's too. *You* killed him, dude. *You* fucking killed Randy!"

Manny's eyes were bugging out with horror now. "Man, I'm sorry, I really am! I didn't mean to—"

Rick wiped his eyes. "Shut up, asshole. Your fate's already sealed. We're gonna do this the old school way—an eye for an eye." Leaning on the shotgun, Rick bent over to stare really closely at his bound friend, sweat dripping off his shaven head onto the lower man. "You and me, dude? Oh, we're still going into the Dark Zone. Just that you ain't gonna be returning."

"You're going to feed me to the gargoyles? Please, Rick, no!"

"Nah, I'm not gonna feed you to the gargoyles. We're just going on a long drive together, that's all. Only, you ain't gonna be riding in the car."

That was when Manny realized that in addition to binding his ankles together, Rick had also connected them by a rope to the Camry's trailer hitch.

"No!" he shrieked. "You can't do this to me!"

Rick began laughing loudly again. "Says who? The US government? This is Hell, bro. Time for you to give the Devil his dues."

"NO NO NO!" Manny shrieked as Rick walked away from him and climbed into the driver's seat again. "NO, RICK, COME BACK AND UNTIE ME! YOU CAN'T DO THIS TO ME! I'M SORRY! I'M SORRY! I'M—!"

But now the car was in motion and he was being dragged along the highway at speed and all he could do was scream and scream and scream as Rick swerved the Toyota Camry back and forth across the road, then pulled into the next turnoff and sped over the river, a maneuver which sent Manny rolling back and forth across the road, and which, in addition to peeling most of the skin off his chest, ripped his left ear clean off his head when his head made glancing contact with the side of the bridge.

Manny wasn't dead, but a good amount of his skin was already missing and he was covered in blood.

But they'd only just gotten started. Rick drove the Toyota Camry up to the mountain wall, wheeled it around, then sped back out to the highway again. This time, the turn around the end of the bridge completely shattered Manny's lower jaw, pulverizing it so that he bit off the end of his tongue and swallowed his teeth. The jaw remained attached to his head, but only just—it was so mangled that it looked like an oversized ear.

Rick saw the bodily damage in the rearview mirror and laughed. "Wow, bro, I'm glad to see you're enjoying this trip as much as I am."

Behind the car, Manny—mangled as he was—wasn't dead yet. Though praying to die, he couldn't seem to pass over from life to death.

He caught flashes of the black sun and gray mountain walls. He felt pain, pain and more pain. As the highway surface eroded the skin, fat, and muscles off of his limbs and torso and also ground against his exposed bones, Manny Bishop's mind was a cauldron of regret. He'd planned and schemed and made this trip; and all for what?

Nothing! I accomplished nothing! Nothing at all!

Rick rode up over another bridge. True, the Dark Zone was right up ahead, but Rick was in no hurry to get there. He intended to take his sweet time with killing his onetime asshole-of-a-friend.

CHAPTER 34

Edie

Yeah, dad was right—I should've stayed a small-town girl and nothing bad would've happened to me.

Edie Forrest picked her cautious way between the town houses. After waking up and finding Duncan gone, she'd waited half an hour for his return. When after that time he'd still not come back, she'd decided to go for a walk and see what the town looked like. She'd thought of visiting the bank to get her ID, but then decided to wait for Duncan's return before doing so.

Edie still felt disoriented by yesterday's transition to 666. And she realized she must have been incredibly tired too—the way she'd dropped off after that orange juice she'd had.

I should've stayed in Marietta and become a schoolteacher. But no, I had to become an accountant, visit the big city, see the wide world. And out there in the big wide world I met handsome but greedy Duncan White, and let myself be seduced by his good looks and the lure of ill-gotten gains, and now here I am!

She stopped walking. *Where am I?*

On leaving the Hellton, Edie had at first walked downtown, towards the pink haze that obscured this end of Route 666. She'd wanted to see where the highway ended. But there were few people out and about, and bloodstains everywhere from that morning's ruckus, and after a while Edie had found herself alone on the highway.

Her sudden isolation had made the pink haze up ahead seem scary, as if it was blood dissolved in water vapor. It hung like mist and spray obscuring a waterfall; a great way to block off the end of the world one lived in.

Not daring to investigate it further, she'd turned and headed back toward the town center, this time stepping off the highway and walking between the houses.

Most of the houses she passed were empty, and through the gaps between the buildings, she occasionally saw the river. She didn't need to see it to smell it though. The river smelt horrible, as if a million nameless things were rotting inside it.

And now I'm here with Duncan. I'm sure he's mad at me. He may even feel like killing me for causing us this. But . . . until we find a way out of here—if there is one—we're going to have to work together . . . both as friends and lovers. We both need to be realistic about our current situation. It's the only way we'll survive here.

Edie walked on. She'd now arrived back in the occupied portion of town. Occasionally she heard voices; people laughing or arguing. Once she heard loud passionate moaning.

She giggled. *Some things never change.* She found the lovemaking noises reassuring in their normalcy.

Then through the gap between two adjacent cottages, she saw into the yard behind them and gasped.

In that yard a naked man was hanging from a gallows. His hands were tied behind his back. His face was purple from the pressure of the rope around his neck and his tongue was dangling from his mouth.

He hadn't committed suicide or been murdered though. A woman knelt in front of him, sucking on his stiffly-erect penis. She was taking her time, licking along the swollen organ, occasionally stopping to suck on his testicles. Above her, the man twitched and gasped for air.

Then the woman quickly slipped a short stool under the man's feet. Once he was standing on it, she loosened the rope around his neck, then resumed fellating him.

"Oh, Louise, you're the best," he gasped. "Yeah, suck it like that!"

Edie slipped quietly away. *That's just sick,* she thought. *I've read about scarfing but . . . oh, that's just sick!*

She walked on. Soon, she could see townsfolk moving between the buildings and parked cars. Not feeling like speaking to anyone, she walked out between the next houses so she was beside the river.

But even here sex caught up with her.

She was kicking loose rocks at the oily water surface, when a gasping noise called her attention to the window she was approaching. The window was wide open; sounds of erotic delight flowed from it like water trying to join the dark river. The lady making the noises seemed certain that no one ever came this way.

Edie peeked in. Her eyes widened even more than they had while viewing the man whose wife had been hanging him.

It's the mayor . . . and the sheriff! What . . . !?

Mayor Thornwood was naked and seated on a couch with her legs spread wide. Her massive breasts were exposed in all their glory, and her nakedness also revealed another, more masculine endowment.

She's got a dick! She's a transsexual!

Mayor Thornwood had a stiff penis. Her left hand was wrapped around her erection and she was masturbating herself and moaning in ecstasy . . . while Sheriff Hook had the stump of his right hand—Edie could see his gleaming metal hook on the table beside them—Sheriff Hook's right forearm was stuck almost elbow-deep in the mayor's distended anus. He pulled it out—it looked greased with Vaseline—then shoved it back in deep again.

Edie could only gape at the sight.

"Now you just stick that stump deep inside my ass, you dirty man," the mayor gasped, the pink-nailed hand that wasn't masturbating herself engaged in squeezing her huge breasts, creamy white breasts like huge balls of milk with vanilla-drop nipples. "Yeah, like that—lemme feel it deep in my belly." Her fingers meanwhile played with her penis; stroking it firmly, jerking it fast. "In and out, Hookie, you know just how I like it, honey—slooooow-ly now, slooooowly, man. SHIT! I'm gonna come!"

On that short notice, Mayor Thornwood reached out for a handful of Hook's brown hair and pulled his face up close and personal to her throbbing penis.

"Don't'cha stop fisting me!" she gasped while squirting semen all over his face. She came a lot, covering his face with her love milk from forehead to chin.

While still plumbing his stump in and out of the mayor's anus, Hook licked up the semen as it dribbled down over his lips. Then, her bosom heaving, the busty transsexual mayor leaned forward and began licking her semen off the sheriff's face too.

Disgusted again, Edie padded quietly away from the window. *Doesn't anyone do it normally here?*

Then, giggling at all she'd seen, she moved onward, toward the edge of town.

Ha, ha, ha! Duncan isn't going to believe this when I tell him about it!

CHAPTER 35

Duncan

After walking through 666 for a while, Duncan had at first sat on the front porch of an empty house by the roadside. He'd sat there for an hour, putting his thoughts in order.

Yes, so that's done with. I'm no longer mad at Edie. I no longer want to kill her. In fact, I might even marry the lady if she's not too shrewish.

Duncan had watched the road, the people walking, shopping, turning in and out of 666's side streets: Two pretty women walking dogs; two teenage boys on bicycles, both apparently delighted that there were no schools here; a man loading a rolled up carpet into a pickup truck across the road. What Duncan saw reinforced his previous impressions. This place could simply be just another small American desert town. It had a bank where he and Edie could work, or they could fit in somewhere else.

All in all, Duncan White had felt optimistic about the future. *We seem to have been shunted sideways, out of the rat race.*

He'd seen the scary mess in the hotel parking lot, however. Someone had told him that those splattered remains were those of the just-arrived dentist, and also explained how the old man had wound up like that.

Those gargoyles—or 'goyles as the town residents call them—are a major pain in the ass.

It was while he'd been thinking this that one of the gargoyles had flown past, right in front of him, with a shrieking woman clutched in its claws.

Duncan then had his first sight of one of the hellish creatures—an apelike body that was black as night, with huge wings like smears of melted tar and a round head that seemed like a ball of pointy teeth.

The gargoyle looked briefly in his direction before sweeping upward. Its amber eyes clawed Duncan's mind with their frightening gaze.

Fearing lest there be more of the monsters around, Duncan had leapt up and dashed into the house. He'd slammed the door behind him, and stood shivering with his back to it. He'd felt like he'd empty his bowels into his trousers; he'd clenched his buttocks tight to avoid doing so.

I remember that girl! She lives in the hotel too!

***

Now, about ten minutes later, Duncan got control of himself. He hurried over to the living room window and peeked out. The road outside was devoid of life. Like himself, everyone had clearly assumed the gargoyles were back for a second raid today.

But the skies seemed clear enough.

Still, Duncan now needed to use the toilet. He looked through the house, finally settling on the small but comfortable toilet just off the hallway. The water was running, but he didn't have any toilet paper. After some thought he decided to wipe his ass with his underpants and discard them afterwards.

He dropped his pants, sat on the toilet, and gripped his belly as the fear-loosened excrement exited his body in a stinky rush.

"Shit!"

Then someone knocked on the toilet door.

Duncan trembled on the toilet seat. *Did I actually just hear that?*

The knock came again.

"Hey, is someone in there?" It was a man's voice, but eerily, it seemed to be coming from farther away than the corridor outside the toilet.

"Yeah," Duncan replied. "Sorry, I didn't know anyone was home. I thought the house was empty."

"Oh, that's alright. I'll wait till you're done."

Duncan didn't hear the man departing, so he assumed he was waiting outside the toilet. The man didn't say anything else though, so Duncan got on with emptying his bowels. It was embarrassing to be caught using the toilet without permission in someone else's house, but he'd apologize properly once he was through.

Then thirty seconds later, he heard the voice again. "Hey, buddy, you alright in there?"

"Yeah," he grunted. "Be out soon."

Then he froze in shock: *The voice! It came from right behind me!*

"Hey, buddy, how's that shit coming along?" the person behind him asked.

Duncan slowly turned his head and looked behind him.

God! No!

There was a face on the wall. The face was jet-black in color and seemed smeared over the wall. It had a bulbous nose, slit-like red eyes and a wide, stretched-out mouth filled with horrible metallic teeth.

"Hey, buddy, I asked, how's that shit going?"

Duncan was already in motion, leaping off the toilet, but the face on the wall was faster. It shot out a long black tongue that snared Duncan around the neck and dragged him back. The tongue had spikes that pierced into his neck and drew blood.

"Please!" Duncan pleaded with the monstrosity behind him. "Let me go! I didn't mean to shit in here! Let me—YEOW!"

A horrendous agony had just shot through his behind. With the creature's tongue wrapped tightly around his neck, he looked down at the toilet seat and gaped in terror. His buttocks were missing. The entire toilet seat and bowl had now transformed into a yawning black maw that had bitten his ass off. Stripped bone remained where his buttocks had been. Blood was streaming out of the hole in his skin.

In uncomprehending horror, Duncan looked back at the face on the wall, the mouth of which was grinning broadly.

Then, as pain once more ravaged his waist area, he gaped down again.

This time the toilet creature's mouth was completely wrapped around his hips, so that he seemed to be sitting inside it.

He screamed as it crunched down on him again. Now, his entire waist region detached and vanished into the creature's mouth. His severed legs fell to the floor. With no lower body left, Duncan's guts all slopped out of him onto the chewing black lips.

The next time the horrendous infernal mouth yawned open, the tongue wrapped around his throat let go of him, so that he dropped straight down into it.

Duncan was already dead by now, but his spread arms prevented him falling all the way into the monster mouth. However, this proved no problem for the creature: a bite through his chest, and his head and shoulders slipped through easily enough.

"Yeah, buddy, you really should watch where you shit next time," the shadow-thing laughed as its lower mouth fed.

Then it extruded tentacles that picked Duncan's severed legs up off the floor, and it ate those too.

CHAPTER 36

Rick

Rick parked the Toyota Camry, got out and walked round to the back of the car. He smirked down at Manny's remains. "In your next life you'll be careful who you shit on, asshole."

By this point, after two trips up and down the highway, there really wasn't much of Manny Bishop remaining. His head was gone, as were both of his arms and most of his torso, but his hips and legs were still attached to the car. His buttocks and crotch were ground down to sheets of bone, and his thighs weren't much better, but his feet, shins and calves, all of which had been elevated from the ground during most of the drive, were still intact.

"Shit, dude, and all for nothing. 'Cos we were your friends. If you'd asked us, we'd have come willingly. That's what friendship's all about—to be there for each other. But no, you had to go and . . . shit!"

Rick spat on Manny's remains, then cut them loose of the trailer hitch. After some thought, he picked Manny's legs up by the rope and dragged them after him, his other hand carrying the shotgun. Pearl's revolver was stuck in his waistband.

He stepped off the highway and headed into the Dark Zone.

Sunlight glinted off Rick's head as he walked. He'd parked the car about a mile deeper into the Dark Zone than they'd driven in yesterday in the SUV.

So far he'd seen no sign of the gargoyles anywhere. But the buildings were creepy enough, both from the aura of bygone days they projected, and from their look of ruin and disrepair and reek of rot and mildew. And this before he'd even stepped inside any of them. Dark broken walls, cracked and glassless windows, and caved-in roofs were all around him.

Here too, the air was dimmer, sunlight seeming not to penetrate properly to the ground; creating a twilight world, one as unwelcoming as a swamp at dusk.

Rick stared up ahead, at the fog of swirling darkness that seemed alive. He thanked God that Al Gore didn't live in there. Because if he did, Rick might have quit on his current quest.

Rick had decided to go rescue Minx anyway. The girl wasn't to blame for Manny's stupidity. And besides, Rick didn't feel right about not doing anything to save her. The townspeople's acquiescence to Al Gore's rein of terror had to stop, and Rick, feeling hyped-up and not a little crazy after killing Manny, believed he might be the one to stop Al.

The guy can't just run roughshod over everyone like he likes.

After a while of walking, Rick decided that the gargoyles had to be on the other side of the highway. He'd been dragging Manny's legs along as a diversion if they attacked, but now he ditched them. The burden was slowing him down.

He moved much faster now, losing some of his bravado the closer he got to the black swirl that ended this end of Route 666.

Then, just when it looked like his rescue mission might lead him into the blackness after all, he spotted his destination over on his left: a crumbling white 19th Century two-story building with a van and pickup truck parked beside it.

The legend 'AL GORE'S WHITE HOUSE' was painted in red over the front door. The red just had to be blood.

On the left side of the house, ten yards from Rick, stood a heap of human remains. Most of the remains were stripped skeletons, but there were a few disconnected body parts that looked fresh. Rick gagged when the wind brought the stink of rotting flesh to him.

He hid behind a large rock and considered his next move.

No one's said anything about Al having any assistants . . . other than the gargoyles. So it should be just him and Minx in there. Assuming she is in there and that that hell-bird didn't carry her off to eat her. But Pearl seems to think that Al wants Minx back to rape and torture her some more so . . .

After checking the sky one last time for gargoyles, Rick dashed over to the front door and let himself into Al Gore's house.

The door opened easily. Al clearly felt confident that no one would visit him unannounced.

Inside, the house was a mess, as if it hadn't been cleaned in two years. The walls were grimy and the furniture bloodstained. The smell in the house was atrocious. If the corpse pile outside had stunk bad, the building itself stunk ten times worse. Now Rick really had to work against throwing up.

Stepping farther inside the house, Rick quickly located one source of the terrible smell—a headless flyblown corpse sitting upright in one of Al's living room chairs. It was a man's body, and seemed to have been skinned before being left for the graveworms.

Rick tried crossing himself, but found that for some reason he couldn't complete the gesture. He tried again, with the same result: his hand would form the upright part of the cross symbol, but not the horizontal line. Each time he tried to complete the cross, it felt like something evil got a hold of his hand and altered its direction of motion, either upward, downward, or forward.

Now scared and puzzled, Rick quietly searched the ground floor rooms for Al. Most of the rooms were empty, but one of them was . . .

Staring into that rear bedroom, Rick couldn't imagine a more horrifying sight. Severed human heads were nailed in a circle on one wall, another headless corpse was laid out on a table, and yet more severed human heads lay about the floor, which was itself a carpet of crawling maggots. The stink of decaying flesh from this bedroom was what filled the house. It made the house smell as if it was decaying.

Rick puked in the doorway. *I don't believe this. If this guy's planning on becoming a demon, the demons have the right candidate.*

Al wasn't in this room though, or anywhere else downstairs.

The madman was clearly home, however, as his vehicles were parked outside.

Rick quietly climbed the stairs.

CHAPTER 37

~~Meat~~ *Meet Al Gore*

Rick found Al Gore in an upstairs bedroom.

The man was naked, kneeling on the bed and about to rape Minx. Minx was lying on her back but wasn't tied up. She seemed both frightened and excited.

"Now you're gonna get what you deserve, you damn slut!"

Rick had almost stepped into the bedroom before he noticed them in it. Now he retreated a pace and peeked inside.

Rick was surprised to see that Al Gore had no ears, just a dark patch of scar tissue on either side of his head. He had black hair, was of average height and was muscular, with a forming pot belly. He looked to be about forty-five years old.

Just your average homegrown psycho, Rick thought in disgust. *Ed Gein in a realm where insanity is approved of.*

Al sank his erection into Minx's sex and began thrusting, while she feigned pleasure. "Yeah, take that, you whore! How's this big dick feel, huh, you hell-slut!?"

Then Al began slapping Minx, while she mewled in pain. Rick was about intervening then, but he controlled himself. The young lady was a hooker, was used to getting fucked when she wasn't in the mood; this wasn't too different from her normal life. And besides, for the next five or ten minutes at least, Minx wasn't about getting killed; except of course, Al planned on strangling her during his orgasm.

Rick would stop Al then, but in the meantime the intercourse gave him time to plan.

Al hit more hard slaps to Minx's face that snapped her head from side to side, while she moaned and spat at him. "I bet all those weaklings back in 666 don't give it to you like this, bitch!"

Images of the human heads nailed to the wall downstairs swam through Rick's mind.

Shoot him! Shoot the fucker! Rick's better instincts yelled at him. *Kill him now while he's raping Minx. End him here and now while you've got the advantage!*

But Rick didn't shoot Al. Instead, thoughts of personal glory filled his head: *I'll be a hero! I'll tie him up and take him back to town and let the townspeople put him on trial. Too bad that there's no phones here. I could just have called the mayor to let her know I've captured the local bogeyman!*

Finally though, he got tired of watching them having sex and stepped into the bedroom.

"Hey, no ears!" he growled at Al. "Get off the lady and stand back."

"What the . . . !?" Al exclaimed. But he got off of Minx.

Minx immediately jumped down from the bed and hurried over to Rick's side. She kissed him on the cheek. "Thanks for coming to my rescue!" she gushed in relief. "None of those cowards in town would dare challenge Al. Hey, where's Manny? Didn't he come with you?"

"Manny's outside in the car," Rick lied. "He's on sky-watch for the 'goyles."

Then he returned his attention to Al. "Alright, asshole. Get down off the bed and stand back against the wall."

Al did as instructed. He didn't speak, just stared at Rick with cold gray eyes. The look in his eyes made Rick shiver. Not because he seemed nutty, but because he didn't. Al Gore seemed sane—that was the scary thing. He seemed very normal.

"What are you gonna do with him?" Minx asked. "Are you gonna shoot him?"

Rick shook his head. "Nah, I'll take him back to town. Mayor Thornwood and Sheriff Hook will be delighted to string him up in the town center."

At that statement, Al Gore began laughing. "You and whose army are gonna take me to town, boy?" His laughter grew even louder.

"I ain't joking, man," Rick said. "You're coming with me. You've a whole lot of atrocities to answer for."

"And who are you, son? The FBI? Or Hell's Interpol?"

"Fuck you, man. Yes, *I am* damn well taking your psycho ass back to town with me. You can either come along willingly, or I'll take you there in the sort of bits you make of your victims."

"No you're not," Minx said from behind him. "You aren't taking Al anywhere."

"Huh?" Rick turned to face her, but then something hit him in the back of the head and knocked him out cold.

CHAPTER 38

Rick, Al & . . .

Rousing. Waking partly, with a headache that seemed to come from Hell. Waking up fully and remembering that he *was* in Hell. More recollections dripping in like rain through a leaking roof; these ones memories of how he'd fallen unconscious.

Suddenly, Rick was fully awake again and scared.

He was downstairs, stripped naked and tied to a steel table in one of the rooms he'd earlier searched. Thankfully, he wasn't in the room with the heads on the wall.

Beside the table, Minx and Al Gore had resumed the sexual activities he'd interrupted. Minx was on her knees fellating Al, who'd now put on a pair of jeans, but had his fly open.

"Oh shit," Al gasped, leaning on Rick's leg to steady himself. "Ain't no girl I know sucks dick better than you do, baby!"

Baby? Aw heck! Rick realized he'd been suckered. Minx and Al were lovers.

But that wasn't what really scared Rick and made him feel like his balls were being sucked up into his belly. No, what terrified Rick Pierce now was something quite different.

Minx looked different now.

Yes, she still had the same face with its devil-may-care expression, but she also had wings and a tail, elfin ears, and her skin was furry and a reddish-brown in color; and she had long black claws at the ends of both her feet and her hands; hands which were now coaxing Al Gore to orgasm in her mouth.

"She's a demoness! Minx is a demoness!" Rick groaned to himself as Al went stiff against the table and ejaculated down Minx's throat. "I drove into the Dark Zone to rescue a demoness!"

CHAPTER 39

The Why Of Things

"Manny's girlfriend died five months ago," Minx explained. "Al needed her head, so . . ." The demoness licked a remnant of Al's semen off her palm. "Then we came up with the idea of me impersonating Minx, so I could keep up with developments in town and warn Al about any follow-up posses. It was easy, I'm used to doing body transformations. I actually look like this . . ."

Like red wax melting and reforming, she altered her face till it was almost cat-like, then when Rick nodded, returned herself to looking like Minx again.

"So, Al slashed me up all over," she went on. She grinned, revealing long canines, and looked fondly over at Al, who was now sitting in a steel chair and studying Rick with those cold eyes of his. "That part was fun actually, 'cos we did it during sex. He slashed me up really good, then I wandered off to where Ned Shriver would find me bleeding during one of his hopeless forays up and down the highway looking for the exit from here."

Rick nodded. "So you're really Al's girlfriend."

She nodded back. "In a way. I'm actually his familiar—I'm the demoness he made his deal with and I hang around to help him out from time to time, and also to keep him in line if he considers double-crossing us." She glanced tenderly at Al again. "But I'm very fond of him so we're dating."

"And the lady gives fantastic blowjobs," Al said.

Rick had exactly the same problem as before with Al Gore. The man didn't seem crazy. But all those heads he'd nailed to the wall and his long history with the 666 townsfolk clearly told a different story.

"So, if you're dating, why'd he have the gargoyle kidnap you then? I've already worked out that whenever you leave town to go 'find yourself' like Pearl says, you're really out here shacking up with psycho boyfriend, right?"

"He's not a psychopath," Minx said. "Al's possibly the sanest person down here."

"With all those severed heads next door?" Rick retorted. "Even Jeff Dahmer would be considered saner."

"That's a good joke," Al said. "Me insane. That's a great joke, kid."

The way he said this made Rick adjust his impressions of his captor again. Sure, Al Gore might not be insane, but he was definitely an unpleasant person. Not the kind of man any child would want as their father; or a woman want as her husband.

"We're getting ahead of ourselves," Minx said. "You asked me a question, Rick. The answer to why Al send that gargoyle to pick me up, is that I was late for our appointment this afternoon. Seeing as how I'm supposed to be Manny's long-lost girlfriend, I couldn't just leave him, claiming I wanted to go find myself today, could I?"

Rick looked over at Al Gore. Al shrugged back. "Not just for sex, I assure you. I wanted to show her my progress on our project."

"And he's cracked it," Minx said in delight, looking at Al with utter admiration and smacking her red palms together.

Rick decided they were both nuts. He needed to escape from here quickly before he joined Al's other sacrifices. But with his hands and legs tied to the sides of the table, getting away would require some help.

"But back to what I was explaining," Minx went on. "If I'm Manny's girl, I've no excuse to run away when we've just found each other again. I should be ecstatic, right?"

"Usually, once she's out of town and out of sight of anyone, she transforms to her true form and flies over here," Al finished for her. "When she didn't arrive on schedule this afternoon, I sent the gargoyle to pick her up. I just never figured on anyone being foolhardy enough to actually drive down here to *rescue* her." Al suddenly looked uncomfortable, as if he'd remembered something. "Hey, babe, I'd better go out to his vehicle and fetch the other kid."

Minx shook her head and waved a taloned hand at Al. "Don't bother, darling. The other one's dead."

Al Gore looked less than sure. "Are you sure?"

"I'm sure."

"How d'you know that?" Rick asked her.

"I heard it in your voice earlier when I asked you about Manny. You hesitated before replying. You were scared to tell me what happened. Am I right?"

"Yeah, he's dead," Rick quickly agreed, hoping they wouldn't ask him for details of how the betraying scumbag had died. He could almost laugh at the irony of it all: Manny bringing them to 666 to find a girl who was already dead and was being impersonated by a demoness. Poor deceiving SOB never even knew he was being deceived himself.

Rick squirmed on the table. He decided to try and bargain his way out of his predicament. "Hey, Al, look, man. You just said you've already succeeded in your project. So, if you've successfully convinced Minx that you're worthy to join the unheavenly host, you don't need me anymore, do you? I mean, dude, you never actually needed me in the first place. So how 'bout if you and I strike a deal?"

Al Gore smiled. "I'm listening."

"How 'bout if you let me go, and I promise to keep my mouth shut about Minx here being one of the demons? Besides, with you about becoming a demon yourself, it ain't as if you're gonna be hanging around 666 anymore, right? So it's a win-win situation for both of us, and then—"

Rick stopped talking because both Minx and Al Gore had simultaneously burst into laughter.

"Er, what's so funny?" he asked after a while. "I'm serious. If you let me go, I'm not gonna tell anyone what I've discovered. Besides if I do, you can always ambush me with a gargoyle, can't you?"

Rick had never imagined that a demoness could cry, but the red-skinned Minx was wiping tears of mirth from her eyes. She was laughing that hard. As was Al.

Rick didn't get it. "What's so damn funny, you guys? You might as well share the joke with me."

Minx finally got some control of herself. "It's what you said," she said, her wings spreading out to balance her when an abrupt resurgence of her hilarity threatened to topple her over. "That's what's so funny."

"But it's true, ain't it? He's collecting heads to join you demons?"

Calmer now, the red demoness shook her head. "No, he's not trying to become a demon. Actually, it'd be more correct to say that we demons in 666 are trying to become human."

Now Rick was really confused. "Girl, you've lost me."

Al spoke up. "Rick, I'm not trying to become a demon."

"So why all the bloodshed and killing then?"

"A necessary expediency."

Minx grinned. "What Al's actually been trying to do, Rick, is to unlock the door out of here." She nodded at Rick's shocked look. "Yeah, he's been trying to open the door out of 666."

"And now I've succeeded," Al Gore said, clearly trying not to look proud of himself.

***

"Al came to us demons requesting a way to get him out of here," Minx explained. "He didn't ask to join us—he just wanted to leave this place. So we gave him Volume 666 of the LOTUS—the Library Of The Unholy Sciences. In exchange for payment, of course."

"Damn book cost me my damn ears," Al said, while scratching his right ear-scar. "It's a wonder I can hear anything at all now."

"His ears were delicious," Minx said. "I wish he'd let me eat some more of him, but he refuses."

"They also had me kill the preacher," Al said. "Doing that was almost sufficient compensation for losing my ears."

Minx nodded. "And we're all *very* grateful that you got rid of that holy piece of shit for us." Then she frowned. "Darling, stop interrupting me. Anyway, where was I? Yes . . . so, we gave Al Volume 666 of the LOTUS. There's a spell in it to open a portal out of 666 and—"

"Why didn't you demons open the gateway yourself?" Rick asked.

"A human has to do it. We've tried, didn't work. Anyway, that's why Al's been killing people. The portal is called the 'Headway' because it's made of human heads."

Al took over: "Thirty-six human heads to be exact." He nodded calmly at the horrified look that stole over Rick's features at this revelation. "Yeah, it's a lot, son, but it's like that old eggs-and-omelet saying, you know? I actually had to kill a lot more people though. More like around sixty people, in fact."

Minx nodded. "That was really the gargoyle's fault, darling—the way they sometimes accidentally ripped off a person's jaw or lips or ears while transporting their head over."

"But why so damn many?" Rick gasped.

She leaned over Rick; now he smelt the muskiness of her demon flesh, a reek akin to damp kitten. "It's infernal numerology, man. Thirty-six is six times six. It's also twice eighteen, which is six plus six plus six. And Al also needs a few spares in case a head splits open while he's nailing it to the wall."

Al sighed. "And now the Headway is complete, the exit door from this hellish place built."

"So everyone can go home?" Rick asked. "We can all leave here now?"

Minx shook her head. "Not everyone, sweetheart. One of the rules about this place is, it needs a particular number of residents—human or demon—to keep it open."

"But some of us are definitely getting out," Al said. "I've a wife and kids to get back home to. I left home seven years ago—my oldest girl will just have graduated high school." He scratched the side of his head again. "Still don't know how I'll explain the loss of my ears to Helen though."

"And you demons? What do *you* get out of this?" Rick asked Minx.

"We want to leave here too."

"Why? What do your kind want on Earth?"

She grinned and stroked his shaven head with her claws. "What the legend says is, that any demons who can escape from here to Earth will be granted human bodies; we'll become flesh and blood. We'll lose both our demonic nature and abilities, but in place of that we gain the chance of reconciling with God and going to Heaven when we die."

"You really believe that?"

"It's worth checking out. I lived in Heaven once before the Boss got us kicked out. Up there is way better than down here, that's for sure. For one thing, there's air-conditioning." She laughed. Behind her Al groaned.

"Al still doesn't believe Heaven exists," Minx explained. "Or God for that matter."

"He believes in the Devil, but not in God?" Rick asked. "How's that even possible?"

Minx shrugged and gestured to Al. "He's right here; ask him yourself."

"Let's not get into that again," Al said grumpily. "I just wanna get out of this place—I don't give a shit about what comes after this life." He got to his feet.

"Where are you off to, darling?" Minx called as he strode to the door. "Surely you aren't angry at our discussion?"

He waved back disinterestedly. "No, it's not that. I just remembered that I have to calibrate the heads correctly. They're still slightly out of alignment."

"It *doesn't* work? But you said it does now."

He shrugged. "Yes, it works. But you don't want to step through it and wind up downstairs, right in front of the Boss's throne, do you?"

"Uh uh. The less I see of him, the better. And if he finds out we're planning a mass desertion, they'll be hell to pay."

Al performed a mock bow. "So, hell baby, I'll go check on my severed heads then."

"Alright. You do have enough, right?"

"Yeah, I do. This morning's raid furnished me with the final four . . . and a couple to spare."

Minx gestured down at Rick. "Can I play with him?"

Al scowled at her. "Okay, but don't damage his head. Just in case some of the others blow up like last time."

"But, honey, I was so looking forward to eating his ears."

"No. And that's final." With that, Al Gore walked out the door.

Rick was left alone with Minx. She had an evil gleam in her green eyes and was licking her lips.

"What do you mean by 'play with me?' " he asked nervously.

Her red wings spread wide as she replied him: "I'm going to torture you a little. It's been ages since I last tortured anyone. That's the downside of pretending to be human."

Rick began squirming on the table. "Torture? Are you nuts?"

"I'm a demoness. You're somewhere in Hell. That's what we do here—torment the damned."

"How can I be damned? I'm not even dead yet?"

She walked out of sight behind his head, and he heard the tinkling of metal implements. "You'll be dead soon enough, your corpse gargoyle food."

When Minx returned to her previous position by Rick's side, she was holding a small knife in each hand. She raised each blade to her mouth and licked it. Then, seeming to tingle with excitement, she gave each of her furry red breasts a gentle squeeze.

"Can't we just have sex?" Rick pleaded. "That's *real* fun."

Her eyes shone with non-human lust. "Sorry, honey, at the moment I ain't in the mood."

Rick tried to reason with the red demoness: "Listen, Minx, you *can't* torture me. You just said that once you're human, you intend to live a good life and go to Heaven when you die. With that in mind, don't you think God's gonna take a really dim view of you cutting me up just for fun and games?"

Saliva dripping from both of her knives, Minx paused to reason that out.

Finally she shook her head. "Nice try, man, but your logic's flawed. At the moment I'm a demoness. We live by a different set of rules— I can torture you all I want. In fact, it's expected of me; God may even be pissed-off if I don't hurt you. But it's a different ball game for you humans; you're supposed to love one another. Once I'm human myself, I plan on being the cleanest, nicest woman alive. No more sex ever again—down here I've already been fucked enough for twenty lifetimes. It'll be a massive relief not to have to whore myself anymore." She laughed. "I plan on becoming a nun then. I'm gonna shut myself up in a convent somewhere, love God with all of my heart, soul and strength, and pray for the rest of my human life. But now—"

"But . . . but . . . !" Rick protested helplessly as the knives came closer to his belly. "You . . . you . . . don't . . . please!"

"Sorry, man," Minx said, without the slightest hint of compassion in her voice. "Blame Al, not me."

"Wha-what do you mean?" One of Minx's knives was already pressing into the skin of his belly, about to cut through the skin.

"Because of Al's success in opening the Headway, you'll likely be the last person I ever get to torture. So, I need to make the most of this opportunity—get as many thrills from it as I can. You know, so that afterwards I'll have no regrets."

"Noooo!" Rick gasped as the blade sunk into his belly. "Stop it. Stop it!"

"I'm *not* gonna stop it," Minx said, her eyes wide with excitement. She twisted the knife and then pulled it out, smiling at the flow of blood. Rick howled again as she sliced away the skin around the cut she'd made.

Minx frowned at him for a moment, then crossed to the door and shut it. "Since losing his ears, Al's sensitive to loud noises," she explained on her return to his side. "I don't want him messing up his calibration just 'cos you can't endure a little agony."

Rick spat in her face. "Screw you, you crazy bitch!"

She licked the spittle off her face and swallowed it. Her tongue was horribly long. "Now you're getting properly into the spirit of things. Cuss all you like. Okay, let's see what your lungs look like."

"What? NOOOO!"

But Minx was already cutting into him again, this time sticking both of her knives into the right side of his chest. She made two quick incisions, then dug her talons into them. She jerked her hands back. Rick shrieked at the loud snapping of bone and then gaped at what she was holding.

"Just two of your ribs, man," she said, waving the grisly mess in front of his face. She threw the ribs away behind her, then leaned forward over the opening she'd made in his chest. "Nice and pink, just how they should be."

The pain had already rendered Rick speechless. He couldn't even scream when she began poking her knives into his exposed lung.

CHAPTER 40

Pearl & Hook

"Ha ha ha!" Pearl said. "So, the mayor made you suck her cock again. And she made you drink her come too."

Sheriff Hook, his hook-hand back in place on his right wrist, did his best to look dignified. He was used to Pearl mocking him.

"Pearl, it's my damn job?"

"Sucking dick is your job? I thought that was *my* job."

"Keeping Mayor Thornwood happy is my job. You know she does a great job of running things around here. An occasional blowjob is fine with me." He winced. "It's just that I don't like getting fucked in the ass."

Pearl giggled. "Did she? Today, I mean?"

"Nah, I got away. She was feeling a bit tired after the morning's excitement, didn't have the energy for a fuck. She just wanked herself while I fisted her."

"And now you need to come too. So, why didn't you fuck her instead? You gotta admit she's hot as hell."

He rolled his eyes. "Pearl, if my entire right forearm fits comfortably up the mayor's backside, what kinda friction do you imagine my penis is ever gonna feel up that same hole? Yeah, none. Normally she sucks me off too. But like I said, after this morning's excitement, the lady feels a bit under the weather."

Pearl decided she'd made Hook wait long enough. "Okay, so how do you want it. Usual or special?"

"Usual. I just gotta empty my balls after Mayor Thornwood's gotten me all turned on." He looked around inquiringly. "Hey, where's Minx?"

Pearl shook her head sadly. "She got abducted again. Gone for good this time."

The sheriff scowled. "Damn! And the two boys next door?"

"Suicide. They went off to rescue Minx."

Now Sheriff Hook looked really pissed. "Those two cocky idiots! And here I was, thinking we'd found replacements for Slick! And Minx too? Shit!" He scowled at Pearl. "Girl, I think you'd better give me your special. Hearing all this bad news has filled me with huge amounts of tension that I gotta work off."

"Alright, Hookie, wait outside till I call you in."

Hook left the hotel room, stepped over the blood smears on the walkway, and sat on his Harley Davidson, waiting for Pearl to finish her preparations. He felt sexually aroused, impatient and fidgety.

He was also a little worried. Mayor Thornwood had suggested that he marry her. What this meant to Sheriff Hook was that she just wanted the legal right to sodomize him whenever she felt like.

Hell no! I wonder what she likes so much 'bout me. It ain't like I'm the only man in town with a set of buttocks!

For sure, Mayor Thornwood was a beautiful woman, but the way she fucked his ass, it was like she was trying to tear it to bits. Like she wanted to shred it with her dick. She never went gently back there. Not ever.

Besides, rumor had it that the mayor had spent so much time sodomizing Larry Davis, Hook's predecessor as sheriff, that Larry had been glad to be abducted and eaten by the damn gargoyles. That wasn't a fate Hook intended to share.

Hook was still pondering on this when Pearl's door clicked open and she peeked out. "Alright, Hookie, you can come on in now!"

Feeling moody, Sheriff Hook got off his motorbike and walked back through the door.

Pearl had changed her clothes. Now she had on black leather bondage gear and was holding a whip.

"Take your clothes off, you pathetic piece of shit!" she snarled at him.

Hook quickly undressed. Pearl sat and watched him, her legs crossed, her lips curled in a dominatrix sneer around her joint.

Soon, the sheriff was naked, his penis poking stiffly in front of him.

Still sneering, Pearl got to her feet. After cracking her whip twice, she reached under Hook's erection and painfully squeezed his balls.

"Yes, Mistress Pearl," he groaned, "that's exactly what I need now!"

Pearl let go of his scrotum. Then she slapped him hard in the face. Then again. "I didn't give you permission to talk, slave! Now, get on your knees. Down on your knees! Get down! And don't you dare play with yourself until I tell you to!"

His body tense with anticipation, Hook got down on his knees.

After a final drag on her joint, Pearl began whipping him. She whipped him hard, while he shuddered under the strokes of the whip and tried not to scream out his delight at the pain.

"Thank you, mistress!" he gasped on each lash. "Thank you, Mistress Pearl!"

CHAPTER 41

Rick

Rick wasn't certain how he'd escaped. It was a haze, much like Minx's fictional flight from Al's lair.

While the demoness was torturing and mutilating him, he'd been in utter agony. Then, at some point, the agony had ceased and Minx had left him, saying she needed to fly back to town and resume her career of spy.

And then, after Minx had left, Rick discovered that while tormenting him, she'd inadvertently sliced through the leather strap binding his right wrist to the table.

It had seemingly taken Rick hours to free the rest of his limbs and then stagger naked from the house.

He was a mess now, dripping blood both from the hole Minx had made in his chest and from maybe thirty other incisions. Parts of his skin hung from him in flaps and she'd cut off both of his pinky fingers. The only part of him she'd not mutilated was his head.

He was in so much damn pain!

With every step feeling like it would be his last, Rick retraced his steps back to his car.

It wasn't plain sailing. He ducked out of sight as a pair of gargoyles swooped past, headed for, of all things, Manny's remains. Rick watched the hell-beasts tear the pair of human legs to shreds, then take to the air while still fighting over them.

Even in his own torment, Rick managed to smile. *Sonofabitch served his purpose, I guess. Better him than me.*

Rick had been leaning against a shadowed house wall. Now, when he tried to pull away from it, he found that he couldn't. He looked back to see what was holding him in place.

Shit! The wall was rippling like it was made of black muscle. And what he'd thought was a window was now sliding fast towards him, plus it was now full of teeth and was repeatedly snapping open and shut.

Rick pulled away from the wall with all of his fast-fading strength. He escaped the hungry shadow-thing just in time. But he didn't get away from it unscathed. The mouth in the wall clamped shut on the back of Rick's left arm, tearing away most of the skin and muscle on his left upper arm.

Weeping from the pain, his left arm all but useless now, Rick ran the last ten yards to the car. A glance behind showed him the gargoyles already coming for him.

But somehow he made it, sliding in behind the wheel. It was merely good luck that he'd left the key in the ignition. He turned the key; the engine came to life.

The gargoyles, their huge mouths yawning with nail-like teeth, were already descending towards the blue Toyota Camry when Rick put it in motion and sped off down the highway to safety.

He felt like he was dying though. His body felt cold, and he could see white spots dancing before his eyes.

CHAPTER 42

Pearl & Hook

"Yes, slide it in deeper," Pearl Harbor gasped.

Still dressed in her dominatrix getup, she was lying in bed and Sheriff Hook, his back covered with red welts, was fisting her vagina with his stump. It was a tight, slightly painful fit, but Pearl found the stretching sensation fantastic, mainly because, with Hook lacking a right hand, what he was sliding inside her was nice and smooth, if oversized.

Hook slid his stump deeper into Pearl's vagina, halfway to the elbow now. His forearm was creamed with her milky juices. His penis was hard, but when he reached down to stroke it, she grabbed him by his goatee, pulled his face close to hers, and slapped him.

"Did I give you permission to play with yourself, slave? Did I!?" His stump was still deep inside her body, rubbing against her cervix. Each motion of her hips made her tingle deliciously around the truncated forearm.

"No!" The sheriff's eyes were bright with the excitement of his degradation.

She slapped him harder; twice. "Address me correctly, you law-enforcement worm!"

"No, Mistress Pearl!"

She let go of Hook's beard and smirked at him. "I'll let you come only after you've made *me* come, slave. Now, get back to work fisting me! Give me some of what you give our slutty mayor! Do it right, or I won't let you come at all!"

"Yes, Mistress Pearl!"

Sheriff Hook got back to fisting Pearl, fondling her breasts with his good hand. Pearl shut her eyes and relaxed. Despite the slight discomfort, this was nice. It was very nice indeed.

She wasn't certain which of them was enjoying this more. Yes, she was satisfying the sheriff's masochistic urges, but she was really getting off on this too. The feel of his stump inside her—touching every expanded fold of her sex—was magical. She also felt purged by the whipping she'd given him, as if she'd been hoarding violence inside herself for ages and had needed to release it. Expressing herself this way, through sexual violence, was definitely helping her cope with Slick's death, and also with the loss of the two young men who'd driven off into the Dark Zone on a suicide rescue mission.

Pearl Harbor was about to climax when a loud 'Bang!' sounded outside the room. It wasn't just a noise either. She felt the shockwave of a heavy impact through the walls.

She opened her eyes in alarm. The front wall was still intact.

"What the hell was that?" she asked Hook.

"Sounded like a car crash," he replied. "Right outside the room."

Hook pulled his forearm out of Pearl's vagina and hurried over to peer out of the window.

"It's your car," he informed her over his shoulder. "It hit the balcony support pillar. One of those newbies—the shaven-headed one—is in the driver's seat."

"That's Rick," Pearl said. "He made it back then."

"But he's covered in blood, and looks dazed as hell. Shit! Back to work."

They dressed hurriedly and hurried outside. The hotel parking lot was deserted. Out on the 666 highway, those pedestrians who'd noticed the crash had already lost interest in it.

The Camry had knocked Hook's motorbike over. He ignored the Harley for the moment, instead heading over to the driver's door of the car.

Hook and Pearl both gasped when they saw how slashed up and bloodied Rick was; with lots of his skin hanging off him in flaps. The young man's eyes were shut and he was breathing weakly.

"What the hell happened to you?" Hook asked.

Rick opened his eyes and turned his head to look at them. His stare was unfocused and his lips twitched.

"Man, who did this to you?" Hook asked. "Who fucked you up like this? Dammit, kid, someone's cut a hole in your chest!"

"Was it Al?" Pearl asked in horror.

"No, it was Minx."

The sheriff frowned. "Minx? Shit, man, did you try to rape her? I already warned you guys about harassing our girls. If you like pussy a lot, just become sex workers like the mayor advised and you'll have more slit than your dick can fill, but—"

"No no!" Rick gasped weakly. "Minx is a demoness. She's in cahoots with Al Gore!"

Pearl's stare narrowed. "Minx a demoness? Dude, you been smoking pot?"

"Hey, man, just hold on," Hook said. "We'll get you to the doctor and get you patched up."

"No!" Rick gasped. He reached a completely skinless hand out of the car and grabbed Hook's forearm stump with it (the sheriff having been in too much of a rush to first slip his prosthesis on). Hook noted that Rick's hand was now missing its little finger.

"Don't try moving me!" Rick whispered. "I'm dying. I can feel it happening. I won't even make it alive into the hotel room. I thought I might, but . . . Just listen . . ."

"Yeah, we're listening. You say *Minx* did this to you?"

Pearl shook her head. "C'mon, Hookie, there's no way that Minx cut Ricky up like this. I know she's cold and calculating, but c'mon now."

"Just listen," Rick insisted, coughing blood up over his lips. "This is very important. See, I found Al Gore's White House . . ."

They listened, their eyes widening with each additional revelation. Pearl in particular looked horrified.

***

"So what you're saying, is that Al Gore has actually built a working portal out of here?" Pearl asked when Rick fell silent.

Rick didn't reply. Hook waited a while, then checked the young man's pulse.

"He's dead," he informed Pearl. "The kid drove all the way back here to tell us the good news, then he died."

"So what do we do now?" Pearl asked. She'd begun shivering, even though the weather wasn't in the least bit cold.

Hook opened the car door. "First of all we dispose of the evidence."

Pearl gaped at him. "What are you talking about?"

"Just gimme a hand with moving him." Then he looked down at his stump and shook his head. "Hold on while I fetch my right hand."

He left her there and returned to her room. When he stepped out again he was tightening the elbow strap that prevented the hook from slipping off his arm.

"Alright, now let's move him," he told Pearl.

"Okay." She joined the sheriff in getting Rick's corpse out of the car. She was horrified to see how mutilated his entire body was.

"Where are we taking him?" she asked.

"Just to Room 6 over there."

With Hook holding Rick's shoulders and Pearl holding his legs, they carried him down two doors from Pearl's room. The key to Room 6 was in the lock. Hook opened the door and they carried Rick inside.

"Alright, now we gotta get him into the bathroom," Hook said after Pearl had shut the door behind her.

"Nope," Pearl said quickly. "I'm remaining right here by the door. Even without this being one of the forbidden 'six' rooms, I'm scared enough as it is. And besides, you haven't even told me what this is all about yet."

"Okay, okay," Hook said. "Just you wait there and I'll dump the body, then we'll head back to your room and clean up and I'll explain everything."

"Hey, watch it over there! This room's gotta be booby-trapped in some way."

Hooking his hook through the hole in Rick's chest, the 666 sheriff quietly dragged Rick's body over to the bathroom and propped it up in the bathroom doorway. Then, as if he'd noticed something horrible inside there, he quickly backpedaled over to Pearl's side.

They stood there by the door, both watching and trembling, as a thick cluster of black tentacles suddenly erupted through the bathroom door and enveloped Rick's body. In a few seconds the tentacles had completely covered the corpse. There followed a horrible slurping noise, and then Rick's body was pulled out of sight into the bathroom. Next came horrible crunching noises.

Pearl bent over and threw up.

"Yeah, I think we had better leave," Hook said. He opened the door and shepherded Pearl out of there.

Behind them, the nauseating sounds of the feeding shadow-thing filled the air.

***

"I don't believe what he told us about Minx being a demon," Pearl insisted as she helped Hook clean Rick's blood out of the car.

"Men about to die generally don't lie, baby," Hook said. Every now and again he winced from the pain of the whipping she'd earlier given him.

"So you believe him?"

"I dunno, but there's a simple test."

"Which is?"

"Well, if Minx turns up safe and sound again—we'll know Rick was telling the truth, won't we?"

Pearl mused on that for a few seconds. "Yes . . . 'cos how many other people have ever escaped from Al Gore even once, not to mention twice? Statistically it's impossible." Then she frowned. "Hookie, we need to hide the car."

"Huh?"

"Yeah, we do. If Minx does come back and she sees it, she'll suspect we know something."

"She's never struck me as being the most logical woman on the planet, but alright. I'll drive it down to the used-car lot."

CHAPTER 43

Edie

Following the river's course out of town, Edie had been thinking on a lot of things:

No wind or rain.

Bleak desert sand and the omnipresent cacti. The lumpy, misshapen plants just increased the world's unnaturalness, creating worry and tension in her mind.

Overhead, that terrifying black sun. Left and right, twin walls of sky-high stone. Running end to end, the river, which stank as if its oily black water was the corrupted blood of a billion corpses.

I'm locked inside a stone tube or tunnel, with sweet dreams behind me and a nightmare up ahead.

Impressions of this underworld assaulted and troubled Edie Forrest.

By now she'd walked far enough out of town that each house was at least thirty yards distant from its neighbor. She'd spent some time wondering how the houses had all arrived here. Had they been transported here by a process similar to that which had abducted everyone? Or had the people here built them? But if the latter was the case, where then had they found wood to do so without any trees?

Now, looking towards the highway, Edie discovered that she was standing almost opposite the creepy "HELLCOME TO 666! POPULATION VARIABLE!" sign.

With a start, she realized she'd isolated herself from what little civilization existed here. *Oops, I've strayed far enough. I'd better get back into town and find Duncan. Let's get ourselves sorted—*

She'd heard wings. Loud and ominous wing-beats. A fast twist of her head and she saw them heading for her. Hideous black things with huge wings like unrolled sheets of night. As if there was no darkness here because *they* were the darkness. Even at this distance, Edie could make out the glint of sunlight off their long and sharp teeth.

The gargoyles were a hundred yards away, but closing in fast.

I'm fucked! Edie thought in terror, then she turned and ran for her life.

Behind her as she raced for safety, she heard the beating of a cloud of immense demonic pinions that announced her imminent death.

CHAPTER 44

Pearl & Minx

Hook had barely turned the hotel corner and vanished from view in the blue Camry, when Minx walked around the far end of the building.

Pearl just gaped at her. Minx looked completely unharmed.

"You got away *again?*" she asked when Minx reached her. "Girl, you must have the Devil's luck."

"You don't sound too pleased to have me back," Minx said.

Pearl quickly shook her head. "Oh no, it's not that. I'm just shocked to see you alive, that's all. When that 'goyle grabbed you I thought I'd never see you again."

Minx pointed to Hook's Harley Davidson, which was now standing upright again. "Sheriff inside?"

"Nah. He was, but he went down the road to buy some pot."

Minx nodded, then she pushed past Pearl into the room.

"So, how'd you escape again?" Pearl asked, following her inside. "And with your memory intact this time?"

Minx grinned and flopped down on the bed. "Oh, it was sheer luck. Someone—I dunno if it was Ned Shriver—shot at the 'goyle on its way out of town . . . and the fucking thing dropped me. I mean, it let go of me in midair and flew off. I thought I was dead, but then I crashed through a barn roof and got knocked silly instead. I'd have been back earlier if I'd been able to see and walk straight." Her eyes widened. "Hey—where are Rick and Manny?"

Pearl had by now determined that, yes, Minx *was* a demon, and that yes, just as Hook intended, they were going to play along with her—keep faking Minx out.

So, trying her best to look sad (which, considering the amount of death she'd experienced today, honestly wasn't hard) she went and sat beside Minx on the bed and took hold of her hands and stared into her green eyes. "I don't know how to tell you this, girl," she said softly, "but the boys went off to the Dark Zone to rescue you."

Minx immediately looked alarmed. "They did *what!?*"

"Yeah, I know what that means too," Pearl said softly. "No one ever comes back from the Dark Zone. Al and the 'goyles must've killed—"

"How could you let them go!?" Minx's voice was full of hurt. "You should have warned them of the dangers!"

"I warned them not to drive out there," Pearl said. "But you know what guys in love are like. Manny said he'd move Heaven and Earth to get you back again."

"Oh, God, no!" Minx screamed. And then she turned her face into the pillow and began weeping loudly.

Nice try, demon bitch, Pearl thought. *But we're onto you now.*

She watched Minx weep for a while then stepped outside to wait for Hook's return.

CHAPTER 45

Edie

Edie dashed past the nearest house, which looked too flimsy to withstand a demonic siege, and made for the next in line, which seemed built of stone.

How the hell could I . . . ? We were warned to arm ourselves!

Edie looked back once. The gargoyles were almost on her now. Less than thirty yards behind her. Gaining on her fast. She could hear their voices now. They had a horrid squawk that was so inhuman it almost sounded human. She imagined she heard them telling her how much they'd enjoy ripping her to shreds.

She put more effort into reaching safety. By now her lungs felt like they were burning. But if that was the price of staying alive, then so be it.

All I have to do is make it through that front door.

The stone house got closer. She heard her pursuers get closer too.

And then several gunshots rang out behind her.

Startled by the noise, Edie fell to the ground and rolled over. The flock of gargoyles, about fifteen yards away from her now, were reeling back in confusion. Two of the creatures already lay on the desert sand—both seemed dead.

There were more gunshots, and then the man firing at the monsters strode into view. He had a pump-action shotgun pressed to his shoulder and was picking off the gargoyles with the deadly accuracy of an Olympic clay pigeon shooter.

Edie was impressed. Four or five more gargoyles dropped to the ground—most minus their heads—and then the rest of the flock turned tail and flew back towards the Dark Zone.

The man lowered his shotgun from his shoulder and walked towards Edie. She got up and went to meet him. It was Ned, the redneck-looking man she and Duncan had met while driving into town last 'night.'

"Hi, lady," Ned greeted, stroking his long blonde beard. "Hey, you're Edie, if I remember right."

She nodded.

"Lucky for you that I was around," he said. "What the hell are you doing out here? And without a weapon to defend yourself with too?"

"I was looking for my boyfriend and got lost," Edie replied distractedly. She was staring behind Ned, at where the dead gargoyles were fading away into nothingness. Each one of the hellish creatures first turned transparent and then vanished completely.

He realized what she was looking at and grinned. "Forget 'em. Damn fuckers never stay dead for long. Whoever runs this place keeps resurrecting 'em. At least I assume that's what happens. Else I shoulda shot 'em all dead ages ago."

"Thanks," Edie said finally. "I-I really thought I was a goner just now. But-but, Ned, what are *you* doing out here too? I thought everyone here lived in town."

Ned shook his head and pointed behind her. "Not me, lady. I live over there, in the old Acme Bible Church. It's the building behind the one you were headed for."

Edie recalled seeing the church yesterday. "But why?" she asked. "Why do you live in the church when there's safety in numbers?"

Ned laughed. "Church is the safest place there is here. It's the only place the damn 'goyles never visit. The shadow-things avoid it too."

"Yes, but don't you get lonely? And want company?"

Ned nodded sadly. "Yeah, sometimes I do. Occasionally I drive into town for a cool beer." Then he smiled. "But safety ain't the only reason I live there in the old church. That's just the excuse I give everyone. Come on, I'll show you the real reason."

He strode past Edie. She turned and followed him.

Behind them, the last of the dead gargoyles faded away into the air.

CHAPTER 46

Edie & Ned

The Acme Bible Church was a white cottage with black crosses painted on its walls, windows and doors.

"This place is eerie," Edie said as they entered the church yard. "I don't mean that in a bad way though."

"Yeah," Ned agreed. "Maybe God's presence is still here. What I know for sure is that neither gargoyle nor demon dares come near this place." He pointed left. "That's the parsonage where I live."

She looked that way. Ned's reinforced pickup truck was parked in front of a small red-brick building.

They stood for a while in front of the church. Then Edie asked, "So, what were you going to show me here? What makes you live here all alone?"

"Come inside the church."

They walked inside. The interior of the cottage had been converted, with several walls knocked out to form a worship hall. There were two rows of wooden pews and plastic chairs; and down at the front of the nave, a crude depiction of Christ on the cross painted on the wall behind the altar. The preacher who'd lived here might have been a holy man for sure, but he'd been a crap painter.

"Down at the front," Ned directed, leading the way.

Edie followed. Already, since walking in through the door, she sensed something different about this place, but couldn't place the emotions it raised in her. She wasn't religious, so it wasn't a feeling of worship. But what was it then? Peace? Contentment? Calm in the midst of life's raging storms?

Then she smelt the pleasant fragrance of . . . flowers?

"Here we are," Ned said then. "Look!"

153

She could hear—no, she could *feel*—the excitement in his voice. He was pointing in front of the left row of pews, but she'd already seen the burst of violent color over there—blue, yellow, white, red, orange, purple—an authentic rainbow garden of flowers. And their fragrance—gaudy, intoxicating, exhilarating. She breathed in the floral scents deeply—a truly welcome breath of fresh air.

"I know exactly how you feel," Ned told her as she stood there with her eyes closed, luxuriating in something 'normal,' something that wasn't fucked up. "Sometimes I sleep in here and let the fragrance remind me of home."

Finally, Edie opened her eyes. She felt totally rejuvenated. This blooming mini-garden beside her was an affirmation of life.

"This is just wonderful," she said with deep emotion. "Does the 666 underworld have other places like this?"

Ned shook his head. "This is the only place here that's ever had flowers," he said sadly. "Or that'll ever have any . . . 'cept of course, we can find ourselves another preacher to martyr."

Edie gasped and covered her lips with spread fingers. "You mean . . . ?"

"Yeah, the flowers all grew out of the reverend's blood after his death."

"You're serious?"

Ned nodded. "Yeah. Reverend Stevens was beheaded right here while he was praying. Blood all over the front here when I found him. I came back a week later and the flowers had sprouted from the bloody ground."

Edie had no reply to that. On Ned's invitation, she sat on the front pew, and they both reveled in the delightful fragrances. And the colors, the beautiful sunburst brilliance of the blossoms.

Then Ned looked at her seriously. "But please, Edie, keep this a secret. I never told anyone 'bout it before. And the townsfolk are all too scared of the demons' retaliation to come out to the church nowadays. But if they found out 'bout this garden here—they'll likely come out just to pluck the flowers. And I don't know if they'll regrow or not."

"I promise not to mention it to anyone," she said honestly. "Not even to my boyfriend."

"You can come out here anytime you like."

"Thanks."

"Just, next time be sure to bring a shotgun and watch the sky for 'goyles."

She laughed. "Oh, I will, Ned, I will. Thanks for sharing this with me. You've no idea how much seeing this means to me."

CHAPTER 47

Pearl & Hook

"You've got to be kidding me!" Pearl said with a honest-to-god shiver.

"No I'm not," Sheriff Hook whispered. "Keep your damn voice down!"

The pair were having a late lunch in one of the cafés opposite the Hellton. They were the only clients, but the cashier had left his counter and was now watching the street through the café entrance, which was near their table. It was late in the day, 5 o'clock 'in the white' by the café's clock.

On hearing what Hook was proposing, Pearl had lost all interest in her sandwich. She stared at him like he was mad. "You're suggesting that we go over to the Dark Zone and use Al's portal ourselves?"

The 666 sheriff nodded and scratched his goatee. "Why else d'you think I made us get rid of Rick's body?"

"So Minx wouldn't know that we're onto her?"

"Partly true. But the reason for that was so we can get to Al's so-called 'Headway' without any hassles. I wanna leave this damn place and I'm sure you do too. If Al's found the way outa here, we'd be fools not to attempt making a break for it."

Pearl shook her head at him. "You're nuts, Hookie. You're looking to get us both killed."

Hook smiled coolly. He wasn't eating either. "Just hear me out. At the moment, Al may or may not have realized that Rick's escaped. Either way, with the way Minx butchered the kid, he won't expect him to get far enough to tell anyone what he's discovered. And Minx, for her own part, has no idea that we know who she really is. So what's to stop us heading over there and taking advantage of their ignorance?"

Pearl mused on that. "The 'goyles?"

156

"Point, but we'll be armed. Two shotguns. You know how the 'goyles *hate* the feel of metal on their bodies."

"Yeah, yeah." Pearl managed to sip her coffee. "So we just drive in there?"

"More or less," Hook whispered. "Only, we're not gonna take a car or truck. We'll take my Harley; that way we can weave in between the houses and avoid the 'goyles. They tend to mass up where the darkness is thickest, right at the limits."

Pearl nodded and tapped her fingers on the table. "Yes, so even if they see us arriving, we'll be at our destination before they can reach us. Alright, Hookie, I see that part of your plan working. But . . . getting back's gonna be a real bitch. Like playing Russian roulette with five bullets in the revolver."

"Don't you get it yet, girl? We ain't coming back here, ever—we're blowing this damn joint."

"Dude, you sound like a con trying to bust of the slammer."

"This place *is* a prison."

Pearl reached across the café table and laid her hands on his; flesh on flesh, flesh on metal hook. "Alright, I'm with you. We'll break out or die trying." Hearing one of the café's waitresses approaching, she leaned in closer, as if she was about to kiss Hook. "What about the townsfolk? It seems selfish not to tell anyone 'bout this."

Hook nodded. "Yeah, I feel bad about that too. But if we do mention it, there'll be a scramble."

"And the mayor? I thought you were in love with her."

"Maybe I am, but not with her dick. Anal hurts, especially if you do it rough, the way Sally always does."

"That's the reason I don't do anal either."

"It's like she's taking out her frustrations with being here on my butthole." He grimaced as if still feeling one of those unwelcome rear intrusions, then said, "Listen, I'll leave a note explaining everything at the town hall for Sally. That way, she can come investigate after we've left. We're in luck that she feels indisposed to be at work today." He looked searchingly at Pearl. "Ready to go?"

"Yeah! Let's blow this joint!"

They paid their bill and left the café.

***

"We gotta think up a good excuse to tell Minx though," Hook said as they crossed the road back to the hotel. "We don't wanna arouse her suspicions; at least not for the next hour or so. By then, we'll be long gone from 666—in one sense or the other."

"Now you're scaring me, man. Just stop it already."

Then, approaching the Hellton, Pearl spotted Mr. Brooks coming down the stairs from the third floor. "Shit, I forgot we made a appointment for this evening."

"I wonder what bondage position he's prepared for you tonight?" Hook teased. "Touching your toes while he takes your rectal temperature with his meat thermometer?"

"Gimme a break," Pearl scowled. Then an idea struck her: "Hey, Hookie, I know what I'll do! I'll pass the job on to Minx—tell her the mayor wants me for something kinky. She'll buy that." Then she laughed wickedly. "In fact, doing so will be killing two birds with one stone."

***

Hook and Pearl arrived at Room 4 before Mr. Brooks, who seemed to have detoured to the restaurant. They found Minx lying in bed and still pretending to be miserable. They told her what they wanted.

Minx at first protested. "C'mon, you guys, you both know I'm mourning Manny."

"Sex helps you grieve better," Pearl said. "Orgasms help a woman view her sadness in its proper perspective."

Minx looked scandalized by the suggestion, but then, as if sensing the others expected her to give in, agreed to substitute for Pearl with Mr. Brooks. "I'll also be missing my styling appointment at the salon," she pointed out, running fingers through her red locks.

"Oh, you can do your hair tomorrow," Pearl said. "You still look cute. Doesn't she look cute, Hookie?"

"Yeah," Hook said. "Cute as Misty Mundae."

"Alright, I'll do it," Minx agreed, then added, "Well, besides all that, it's hard to mourn the guy when I'm already beginning to forget him again."

Pearl pretended to be surprised. "You're losing your memory again?"

"Just my memories of Manny. It was fine when he was near me, but now that he's gone . . . Yes, I feel like I should be sad, but I can't seem to remember enough about him anymore to feel like I've lost something significant."

"Alright, ladies, he's here," Hook whispered as a knock sounded on the door.

CHAPTER 48

Rope Tricks

Mr. Brooks wasn't upset with the change. Not in the least. His blue eyes shone with lust as he surveyed Minx's nude body on the hotel bed.

"I've heard a lot about you," he said, running his plump fingers along Minx's smooth legs. "The boys all say you've a delectable pussy."

Minx shrugged. "It works, it fucks." Then she looked up at Pearl and Hook. "So, the mayor wants a threesome?"

Hook shrugged. "Or maybe she just wants to watch me and Pearl do it. Mayor Thornwood ain't feeling too good today. I'm doing my very best to keep her entertained."

Minx nodded and spread her legs. Mr. Brooks already had a thick coil of rope in hand and was flexing it.

Pearl watched Mr. Brooks fold back Minx's right leg and bind her ankle to her right wrist. Minx grimaced as he pulled the rope tight, then she relaxed. Then she grimaced again.

"Ouch, take it easy!" she protested.

"Am I hurting you, darling?"

"Yes!"

"Oh." Mr. Brooks made certain the knots were tight enough and then reached into his bag and pulled out a gagball. Minx's eyes widened in fright.

"Now, now, now, darling," Mr. Brooks cooed. "I'm not going to hurt you, not at all. But you have to learn to endure bondage like a big girl. Now bring that beautiful mouth over here and let me stop it up."

Once he had Minx gagged, Mr. Brooks resumed work, folding Minx's left leg back also and binding it to her left wrist. Next, he rolled

Minx over onto her belly and tied her elbows together. Minx lay there looking confused.

"Yes, yes, yes," Mr. Brooks enthused. "This is just your first lesson, girl."

Now, as though he and the redhead prostitute were alone in the hotel room, he undressed completely, then got out a large dildo from his bag. "Alright, darling, let's see how stretchy your ass is. Try to relax. Always remember: big girls don't cry, their holes just get bigger."

Minx's eyes widened with pain as Mr. Brooks began feeding the dildo into her ass hole. As the immense sex toy penetrated deeper, she began squealing: "Mmmph, mmmph!"

Pearl tapped Hook on the shoulder. "I think we can leave now," she whispered. "This is what I meant by killing two birds with one stone. Take my word for it—the bitch won't be going anywhere for two or three hours."

"Hey, let's go," she added when Hook seemed to be showing more than a passing interest in Minx's sexual predicament. "At the moment I feel brave enough to go through with this idea of yours. In half an hour I'll have lost all my courage."

That got Hook moving. "Well, I guess we'll be leaving now, sir," he told Mr. Brooks as he opened the hotel room door. "But you just keep up the good work, sir."

"Sure thing, sheriff." The naked man turned, gave them a thumbs-up, then resumed shoving his big dildo up the bound redhead's backside.

"Mmmmph! Mmmmmmph!" Minx Fortune growled from the bed, saliva dribbling all around the rubber ball in her mouth.

CHAPTER 49

Edie & Ned

"I don't feel like going back to town just yet," Edie told Ned.

So instead, they went for a picnic of sorts. Ned packed some food and drinks and two shotguns and they walked over to the nearby bridge.

"Thanks again for showing me the flowers," Edie said as they spread towels over the barren riverbank soil and sat on them. "Viewing those every once in a while is sure to help me cope with life here."

"My pleasure."

They sat drinking from a six-pack of nameless generic beer. The beer had the same unpleasant undertaste as everything else Edie had tasted here. It almost neutralized the stink of the river.

"So, what do you and your boyfriend do?" Ned asked after a while.

She laughed. "We're both accountants. We work for the same company—Cashstretch."

"Never heard of 'em," Ned replied honestly. "But then I'm from down in Tennessee anyway. USA is such a big place, it's like the left hand don't know what the right's doing."

"Oh, we're a new retail chain. And you, your family? Did you leave them behind?"

Ned shook his head. "My wife Nancy's here. We broke up 'cos she got into BDSM and I didn't feel like being tied up and whipped—felt too much like being tormented in Hell."

"No kids?"

"One teenage son. Rebellious li'l sonofabitch. We'd left him with my sister the Sunday we went missing. I'm sure he's okay. By now he'll be twenty-five. Too old to worry about anymore."

A sudden burst of noise shattered the silence. Startled, they looked around and saw a motorbike speeding off into the distance, white exhaust smoke filling the air behind it. Ned spat in disgust. "Looks like someone's off to commit suicide again."

"Suicide?"

Ned waved a dismissive hand and turned back towards the river. "Forget it, Edie. Let's not spoil this pleasant moment with unpleasant explanations."

He got out sandwiches from the picnic basket, but Edie was already getting to her feet and striding towards the bridge.

"Hey, where you goin'?"

"The bridge. I want to view the water up close."

Ned put the sandwiches down on a paper plate and followed her. He understood Edie's fascination with the river. In his early days here, many were the times when he himself had stood on one of these bridges along Route 666 staring at the Muskingum.

He caught up with her on the bridge and they stood side by side, leaning over the metal railing, facing the town. She was a nice and pretty girl, but Ned didn't feel sexual towards her at all. He felt like she could have been his kid sister April who he'd left his son Kenny with back then. She had the same blonde hair; the same face and posture.

"Ned," Edie said as they stared at the black sludge-like water. "Yesterday you said you've been trying to get out of here for eleven years."

He nodded without looking at her. "That I have. And I'm still tryin' to get out. But it's just been one friggin' disappointment after another. Every now and again I'll think I'm close—but it's like the damn demons are toying with me, ya know? Like one of those damn mirages that populate the desert and play games with thirsty men's minds till they die."

"Games?"

"It'd take me a whole day at least to spin you my tale of woe. Crazy, crazy, crazy. One of the least insane things is how the number of turnoffs lining both sides of the highway keep changing."

Edie kicked a rock off the bridge into the river. "Changing?"

"Like I said, it's crazy. Some days I drive down the highway and there's twenty turnoffs on this river side of the road and fifteen on the other side. Next time—sometimes even later that same day—there'll be sixteen turnoffs on this side of the road and eighteen on the other side. Keep in mind that a change in the number of turnoffs on this side also means a difference in the number of bridges."

"That's crazy."

"Just what I said." He looked angry now.

"How about sailing down the river? It must lead out of here."

He looked at her with admiration. "Yeah, I've thought 'bout doing just that; you know, building a canoe and heading downstream. Thing is, the river flows toward the Dark Zone. And from demon rumors, it's pure agony that way. . . . And besides, boating might be suicidal anyway."

"How so?"

"There's big and nasty things in this God-damned black water. I've caught occasional glimpses of 'em. To my mind, we're lucky they don't come out more often."

Edie shuddered. "What sort of things?"

"Tentacles, teeth, eyes, more teeth, then even more tentacles, teeth and eyes. Dunno if they're demons or more of the shadow-things tho'. I mean, one time I saw one that spat fire at me like a dragon. I ain't never run so fast in my life as I did that day. How do you figure that?"

Edie laughed. "If you're trying to scare me, you're doing a world-class job."

He laughed too. "I'm just trying to get you to be careful here. I like you, Edie—you remind me of my kid sister April."

He slipped his arm through hers and pointed back to where they'd spread their towels. "Forget the damn river, girl. Let's go finish our picnic and then I'll drive you back into town to find your boyfriend."

She let him lead her down off the bridge.

***

They ate their sandwiches.

"This one tastes half-okay," Ned said. "Most sandwiches here taste like there's poop inside 'em. That and whatever meat whoever makes them sees fit to put in 'em."

Edie laughed. "I haven't been here long enough to be an expert on the food, but . . . well, as a newbie, I'm more concerned with the mechanics of this place anyway." She pointed ahead of them, to the endless mountain a mile off. "Like that, for instance. It's like we're trapped in a box. Maybe this entire 666 space is a 'cardboard' box dumped in some cosmic wasteyard and this river is merely someone's spilled oil?"

Ned chewed more of his sandwich, swallowed, swigged beer and nodded at her. "Go on."

"Maybe there's no purpose to any of this at all. I mean, I think there is . . . but, what if we've actually been forgotten here and the demons are just . . . Oh, I dunno. It's all just so weird." She took a bite of her sandwich.

Ned nodded. "Yeah, I know. When I first arrived here, I spent every day wondering why I hadn't gone crazy yesterday or the day before and expecting it to happen tomorrow or the day after, and—"

He stopped talking suddenly and, his eyes bulging, grabbed hold of his throat. "Shit, Edie, something must've got into our sandwiches while we were up on the bridge! Try to throw it up, quick!"

She did what Ned did next, stuck her fingers into her throat and tried to make herself puke. Both she and Ned had flung down their sandwiches and, once the top layer of bread had fallen off, they could now see little black and wriggling things, like liquid worms, crawling out from between the meat and lettuce and tomato slices.

Edie finally threw up, ejecting a black ooze that hung out over her lower lip and dangled onto her chest. Try as she might, the black jelly wouldn't exit her throat completely. So she grabbed hold of what had already left her mouth and tried to pull the rest of it out. It squirmed in her grasp as if alive and her fingers dug into it, releasing a horrible stink as they punctured its surface. She was already terrified; now, in addition, she felt completely nauseated.

She stared at Ned and became even more horrified. In a gush of blood, a weird and jagged limb like a giant insect leg had just burst out of the middle of Ned's face. The claw or whatever it was, was wet and slimy. Moving back and forth like a saw, it quickly slit its way down through Ned's mouth, chin and neck, and opened up his chest like a can opener at work. Blood squirted out from Ned's body as he split open down the front and a mess of tentacles and insecty limbs spilled out of him.

Edie wanted to scream, but couldn't. Her head felt full of something like molten lead. Her thoughts felt like something was killing them; butchering her intelligence and then eating it. In addition to the nauseating black goop dangling from her mouth, she was aware of strange movements inside her body, painful movements as if she was pregnant and about to give birth, only the baby was incubating in her chest, rather than her womb.

A moment later, it was over for Edie too. Two clawed black limbs erupted from her shoulders, then like a giant crab's pincer, came together, chopping her head in two through the middle.

***

Edie collapsed to the sand, where Ned's corpse was already undergoing a sickening transformation, his entire skeleton being forced out through his skin; skin that was now the color of the gray sky; skin which instantly healed all the tears the emerging bones made in it.

The same evil process happened to Edie's corpse too, the seed-thing that had invaded her disposing of her bones as useless, but assimilating the rest of her flesh into its own form.

Finally, the two resulting shapeless gray masses—skin-enclosed bags of liquid meat that bristled with multiple insect legs and pincers—began clumsily wriggling their way down the riverbank and into the corrupted black water.

The river covered the new monsters. Up on the riverbank, Edie and Ned's skeletons waited for someone to discover them.

CHAPTER 50

Pearl & Hook

"I've never been out here before," Pearl said after Hook skidded the Harley-Davidson to a halt behind a crumbling old wall.

"I've been this way just once," Hook told her. "During that first posse to arrest Al." He shook his hook-hand at Pearl. "With this souvenir of that trip, I ain't had much stomach for the drive since then."

They got off the bike. After first determining that there were no shadow-things nearby, Hook hid the Harley Davidson under a collapsed roof. And, just in case they needed to depart in a hurry, he turned the motorbike around, pointing it back towards 666.

Then he stepped over to Pearl, who, shotgun in hand, was staring up at the black sky ahead. Over there the gargoyles were out in number. They filled the air like Wild West buzzards anticipating a gunfight.

"It's a total mindfuck," Pearl said in awe. "A fifteen-mile ride and it's the end of the world."

"Come on," Hook said, setting off. "The sooner we get to Al's place, the safer we'll be. Less chance of the 'goyles intercepting us and making a nuisance of themselves."

"Fear is a really powerful thing," Hook said after they'd walked a short distance between the rundown houses.

"How d'you mean?"

"I'm just wondering why we never sent just one or two people over here to kill Al. You know, have 'em sneak in like we're doin' now. Each time, we sent out a posse instead—and each time we suffered heavy casualties 'cos of the 'goyles. We had no way of knowing that Minx was selling us out to Al. If we'd sent just one or two assassins, she'd never have known 'bout it."

Pearl made a face. "Hookie, without our current motivation, would you ever have made the trip here *alone* to hunt down Al?"

Hook unhooked his hook-hand from the trigger of his shotgun and waved it at Pearl. "Nah, not with this physical memory of that first trip, I wouldn't. I'd be too damn scared. That first day, the entire sky seemed to have become gargoyles. You ain't never seen nothing like it, Pearl—the 'goyles were falling on us like rain. Blood and body parts were flying everywhere. Guys were getting bitten to shreds to the left and right of me."

"So there's your answer right there, man. The fear you just mentioned."

"Come to think of it though," Hook mused, "I might've chanced it if we'd ever had rocket launchers in the gun shop. Blow the bastard to kingdom come from a safe distance away." He shook his head— "Aw, forget it"—then returned his hook to the trigger of his shotgun in case he needed to fire suddenly.

They walked cautiously on.

"You know," Hook said after a few paces, "I could really do with some head right now."

"What!?"

"You know, girl—head . . . a blowjob, fellatio. A pair of hot lips wrapped around the head of my cock would help me clear my head, for sure."

Pearl rolled her eyes at the slate-colored sky. "Man, put those misplaced thoughts out of your head. Don't even head there."

"Hey, babe, you bring any pot along?"

"Not with where we're currently headed; all I took was bus fare for when we're out of here. Man, we need to be clear-headed, else we both may wind up losing our heads."

"Well said," Hook agreed. "I almost got ahead of myself."

Pearl sighed. "Man, let's just proceed cautiously ahead."

"Do you think this'll really work?" she asked as they stepped past an old colonial building which had more shadows than the perpetual daylight should have created.

"I don't know, but I sure as hell intend to find out." He ducked behind a solitary wall and motioned to her to do the same. "That's Al's place up in front there."

Pearl saw the white house in the distance; a crumbling, run-down wood-and-stone construct that looked as if only the forces of darkness were still keeping it standing. "Why're we stopping then?" she asked.

"Plan of attack. We didn't formulate one before leaving."

"Yeah, that's right. So what?"

Hook tugged on his goatee. "According to Rick, the gateway is on the ground floor, so . . ."

Pearl scowled. "Hookie, this ain't an ATF bust. We *know* that Al's the only one in the house—there's no demon bodyguards and no 'goyles either. Meaning we don't need a damn plan. We just bust in there and kick the asshole's butt."

"Alright, but don't get trigger-happy and shoot him."

Pearl made a face. "And why the hell not, if I may ask?"

"We may need him to work the 'Headway' portal for us." Hook shrugged. "Well, at least don't shoot him until we know for sure that the damn thing works."

"Yeah, alright."

"In fact, baby, if we sneak into Al's house now and find him griping about how the portal ain't perfected yet, we'll just sneak right back to town again and check back next week."

"Count me out of any return trips. Just being here now feels like it's using up half of my life expectancy."

They started forward again. After a while Pearl asked, "What the hell is that awful smell?"

"Don't puke, corpse pile coming up."

They emerged from an aisle between house walls, right next to the hill of human bones, then froze, their hearts in their mouths. Human hand clamped between its gleaming teeth, a solitary gargoyle was just rising into the sky from the charnel heap.

They watched the monster fly off into the dark air, then crept silently across the clearing to Al Gore's White House.

CHAPTER 51

The Connection

"Ugh," Pearl said on seeing the headless, worm-riddled corpse in Al's living room. "This guy sure overstayed his welcome at the White House."

"Come on, come on," Hook urged her. "This way—to the back of the house."

The room in which they found Al Gore was the stuff of Pearl's nightmares. As she and Hook peered in through its open door, she was glad that Rick hadn't given them details of this place or she'd never have found the nerve to make the trip.

The problem wasn't just the double circle of heads nailed to the wall. That was horrifying enough, being comprised of the heads of people she knew, a good number of whom she'd even slept with— one of the closest heads on the wall belonged to her friend Slick. But the rest of the room was splattered with gore and rotting body parts which, from their haphazard locations, seemed to have been flung away angrily when discovered to be useless.

Pearl counted at least twenty more severed heads lying about the room. Some of these were clearly old; dried up and shriveled. Others were shockingly fresh. Most were in in-between states of rot and decay. All had spike-holes in their foreheads, as if they'd once been up on Al Gore's wall too.

There were two tables in the room. One of them bore a fresh, eviscerated skeleton: the man's head was intact; both of his thighs, however, were missing large expanses of flesh, the clear result of gargoyle teeth. On the other table lay a number of books and knives, along with beakers and test tubes such as one would expect to find in a lab.

Then there was all that rotting flesh strewn everywhere. Flies buzzed all over the place. Swarms of maggots crawled left and right like living carpeting.

"This guy is one crazy sonofabitch!" Hook whispered.

"My exact thoughts," Pearl agreed. "I don't care what Ricky said, or what anyone else thinks. Al Gore *is* batpoop crazy. Sane people don't do things like this."

They remained outside in the hallway, gazing in. Once, Hook winced from the pain of the lashing he'd recently received at Pearl's hands.

For his part, the earless architect of all the gore stood inspecting his frightening creation, oblivious to their presence. Occasionally he nodded, then twisted one of the heads slightly on its spike.

The double ring of heads that comprised the 'Headway' began two feet up from the floor, and was about three feet wide. With the thickness of the heads taken into consideration the whole morbid construction was about a foot taller than its creator.

The inner ring of heads were all arranged upright, with about six inches of space between them. They were connected to each other by the outer ring, the necks of which were inserted into the spaces between the inner ones. The ring's center was a flat expanse of stitched-together human skin that had clearly been peeled off several people's backs.

"All the heads on the wall are still fresh," Pearl whispered to Hook. "Even the old ones."

"But the damn thing ain't working yet. I sure hope this trip ain't been for nothing."

"Shush," Pearl said. "Listen—he's saying something."

Al Gore had just turned away from the circle of heads. "Well, that just about wraps that up!" he said, rubbing his hands together and with a look of delight on his face. "Time to switch it on and test run it! I wish Minx was here now—I could do with some celebratory pussy!"

"Sicko," Pearl told Hook.

"Stay calm, stay calm," Hook whispered, stroking her hair. "We need him to switch the damn thing on."

"How's he gonna do that? By remote control?"

Hook shrugged. Al, meanwhile, was picking up one of his books. A large volume bound in pink leather. Al was beaming broadly now, clearly anticipating some great event. Hook and Pearl also sensed something in the air, something wicked and yet awe-inspiring.

Once more facing the rings of severed heads, Al Gore began reading from his book:

"S'daeh fog nir y'l sir guoy,
Dae deh t morf wonn ruter!
Rood sih t pu nepo,
D'l'row sih t mor femes aeler.

Dio vehth gu orht em d'nes,
Eci ohc fot ropy mot.
H'tra eo t k'cab em d'nes,
H'taed g nivil fom la ersih t morf raf!"

"What the hell is the idiot saying?" Hook whispered.

"Shush!"

There was really no need for Pearl to have silenced Hook. He was already struck speechless by what was happening in the room. Al's previously dead circle of heads was coming to life. Each head opened its eyes and stared at Al Gore, who smiled back at them, nodding.

Then the heads began to speak. All at once. Drool spilling from their mouths, they intoned in rhythm in thirty-six different voices:

"Eve i lebod oh wu o yemo clew,
Peels ru omor f'k cab su nomm u show,
Eva el ot luos d'na h'sel fru oy era perp!"

"Shit, now what are *they* saying?" Hook growled.

"It doesn't matter," Pearl replied. "Look at the space between them!"

Another needless instruction: her one-handed companion was already gaping at the space between the heads, which had now transformed from a patchwork of bloody human skin into a shimmering glassy surface, through which they could see . . .

"Shit!" Hook gasped. "It actually worked. That's a highway out there, and people driving past."

"And there's grass and trees too!" Pearl said, with tears in her eyes.

"Ha ha ha!" Al Gore was saying. "Now I can get back home to Helen and the kids—too bad I've missed Tammy's high school graduation!"

Pearl couldn't help herself; she began crying. "I can go home! I can go home!"

Her weeping alerted Al Gore to their presence. He spun around and saw them.

"Fuck," he growled. "Sheriff Hook!"

"Hi, psycho douchebag," Hook said. Shotgun covering Al, he stepped into the room and walked towards him.

"Don't shoot me, man," Al pleaded, dropping his magic book back on its table, and raising his hands in a gesture of surrender. "Don't do it, Hookie!"

Hook smirked at the man. "And why not, Al?"

Al indicated the circle of chanting heads. " 'Cos I did it, see? I got the Headway to work! We can all go home now!"

"He's got a point," Pearl said, stepping up beside Hook. "If it weren't for him and all of his killing, we'd still be stuck here."

"Yes, yes, she's right!" Al pleaded. "You gotta listen to her!"

Hook's face creased up in a frown while he considered Pearl's argument. Behind them, both rings of heads were still speaking, getting louder. Now though, there was a slightly discordant note in their chant. The chant sounded darker, less welcoming.

Meanwhile, Al had lowered his hands again and was inching away from them along the table he'd returned the book to.

"Don't even *think* of making a break for it," Pearl said.

Al nodded and stayed put.

"Yeah, you kinda got a point there, girl," Hook finally told Pearl.

Then he returned his attention to Al: "See, man, I really don't like you at all. I mean, you've killed lotsa innocent people, and personally, I feel a deep need to pay you back for the loss of my right hand. But . . . putting all that aside for a moment, shit, man, you've performed a great serv—"

He shut up when Al's head exploded in a blast of shotgun fire.

When Hook's ears stopped ringing, he gaped at Pearl. "What the hell did ya go and do that for?"

Her face white, Pearl pointed to the steel table. "He was faking us out. I saw him reaching for his gun."

Hook saw the revolver she indicated. He nodded grimly. Then he walked around the table and stared down at the headless man. Blood was jetting from the corpse's neck and covering the maggot carpet. "Shit, man, you just couldn't keep your hands to yourself, could ya! And here I was, gonna plead with the townsfolk to not lynch you anymore and yet you *still* tried to double-cross us." He kicked the body. "Goddamned demon-lovin' piece-a-shit!"

Pearl tugged on his arm. He stopped speaking and stared at her. "What, baby?"

She pointed to the Headway. "Look, something's wrong! I think it's malfunctioning!"

They hurried over to the suspended heads, leaving their shotguns within easy reach on the table with the disemboweled corpse.

Now the heads' demonic voices rose and fell stutteringly as they rhythmically chanted:

Eno geb k'ci up d'na sloof yrruh
Nog nimoc sisir case reht
N'rub d'na h's arc l'li wetag ruo noos!

And the heads now also sparked and crackled as if electricity was being conducted between them. Most disturbing of all, the view of the forest and highway visible beyond the ring of heads was flickering.

"What's wrong with it?" Hook asked. "It looks like it's planning to self-destruct."

"We'll have to chance it anyway," Pearl said with a determined look on her face. "I can't quit now, Hookie. I'm going home no matter the fuck what."

"Hey, I think I've figured it out," Hook said.

"Figured what out?"

"Why the portal's malfunctioning."

"Hook, we gotta hurry!" She made to step through the Headway, but Hook pulled her back.

"Wait, you gotta see this—you're gonna love it."

"Shit, Hook! Let's just get out of here!" But she stepped back from the Headway to see what Hook insisted on showing her. She hated looking at all those severed heads, but seemingly had no choice in the matter.

"So what?" she asked. "WHAT THE HELL ARE YOU DELAYING US IN THIS GODFORSAKEN 666 HELL OF A PLACE FOR!?"

"Calm down. Look at the top head. The 'inside-head' right at the top."

"Hey—isn't that Reverend Stevens!?"

"Yeah it is. Try and focus. See if you can make out what he's saying."

"MAN, WE GOTTA GO!"

"Just try, Pearl!"

"HOOKIE, IF THIS DAMN PORTAL SHUTS DOWN AND I'M STILL TRAPPED HERE, I'M GONNA KILL YOU! I AIN'T JOKING!"

"I'll take my chances on that. Just fucking listen."

Pearl listened. She quickly understood what Hook meant. Reverend Stevens' head, the oldest of the lot, definitely wasn't saying what the others were. The lips of the other heads all moved in sync with each other; the reverend's mouth was out of sync with theirs.

For a few moments, the rest of the voices lulled, and in that silence, Pearl and Hook both clearly heard what the dead preacher was intoning:

"Though I walk through the valley of the shadow of death, I will fear no evil; for thou art with me . . ."

Pearl stared at Hook in shock. "You mean?"

He nodded. "Yeah. The demons really fucked themselves in the ass on this one. Al used the preacher's head as a sign of their victory; but once he activated the Headway and the heads came back to life . . ." He gestured with his steel hook. "Well, you can see the result."

The heads resumed their loud dissonant chanting. The welcoming vista beyond them kept flickering like the dark electricity that leapt between them. Now too, there was a burning smell mingled in with the Headway's reek of dead meat.

"It's gonna blow up for sure," Hook said. "You don't mix holy and unholy shit together without destroying the toilet."

"HOOK, WHY AREN'T YOU IN A HURRY TO GET THE HELL OUT OF HERE!?" Pearl screamed at him in exasperation. "WHAT THE HELL IS WRONG WITH YOU!? YOU'VE SUDDENLY FALLEN IN LOVE WITH THIS GODDAMN PLACE, IS THAT IT!? OR IS IT THAT YOU'RE ALREADY

MISSING MAYOR THORNWOOD'S FAT TRANNY DICK AND WANT TO GO BACK AND MARRY HER!?"

Hook shook his head—"Hell no to that last one!"—then gestured up. "The reverend's head winked at me. I think he's holding the portal open till we get safely out of here."

Pearl stared up at the old preacher's severed head. Dribbling drool like all the others, lips moving as it continued reciting Psalm 23 out of sync with the others, it gave no sign of noticing her. The head did seem to have a faint halo of white light hanging over it, but Pearl decided she was imagining that.

"Hell no—I don't believe that at all," she growled at her male companion.

But right as she said so, Reverend Stevens' head burst into flame. As Pearl watched, all the flesh burnt off the old man's skull, leaving just flaming bone. And, no, she'd not imagined it at all—there *was* a halo floating over the skull, a halo of yellow and blue fire. The skull also had a blazing red glow in its eye sockets that, if anything, made it seem more evil than the other thirty-five chanting heads on the wall combined.

And now it wasn't quoting scripture anymore. Now the skull was laughing.

"SHIT SHIT SHIT!" Pearl gasped in fright, grabbing Hook by the arm and forcibly pulling him towards the portal. "MAN, LET'S FRIGGING GO RIGHT FRIGGING NOW, OR ELSE I'M GONNA LEAVE YOUR FRIGGING CRAZY ASS BEHIND IN HERE!"

Hook didn't need any further urging. He'd also noticed the head's scary transformation. "Alright, yeah! Ladies first!"

Pearl was about stepping into the flickering glassy surface, when she pulled back.

"What's the problem?" Hook asked. "Nerves? You want that I should go first?"

"No, no," she said quickly, while dashing past him towards Al's gore-streaked tables, the words tumbling in a rush from her lips. "It just occurred to me that, if this portal self-destructs on our exit, the demons can easily build another one. All they need is another psycho like Al Gore." She grabbed Al's creepy book off its table and brandished it at Hook while rushing back past him. "But not if they don't have this. So we're taking it with us. Alright, Hookie, let's get the hell out of here."

Above her head, the burning skull was still laughing, its laughter now drowning out the voices of the other heads.

She stepped through the portal, tugging Hook after her.

"Hell, yeah!" she yelped on seeing the world ahead of her. This was the real world, the one she remembered from five years ago, with trees and flowers and . . . grass . . . blue sky and clouds. Yes, there were clouds overhead, and the air held the promise that it might rain soon.

"We did it, Hookie! We made it home!"

"Shit, my damn hook's stuck!" Hook growled behind her. "I can't get my hand loose."

Pearl spun round to help him. They'd emerged through the wall of a house. This side of the Headway was just a space in the wall through which Al's demonic laboratory was visible.

Hook was bent inside the portal fiddling with something. "Shit," he said, "it's stuck in one of these fucking mouths. I'd better loosen the straps and—"

That was the last thing Hook ever said. There was suddenly a bright explosion inside Al's house. And then, like jaws closing, the portal snapped shut, cutting off Hook's head and right arm. The wall became just a wall again. Hook's decapitated corpse slid down it, leaving bright streaks of blood.

Pearl could only gape at Hook's body.

"Shit!" she said after a minute.

Then, book of spells gripped tightly, and without looking back, she turned and walked away, around the side of the building.

CHAPTER 52

Pearl

She and Hook had emerged from the south wall of the Red Eagle gas station convenience store on Route 666. The position of the station dumpster, also on that side, meant Hook's corpse wouldn't be visible from the road.

Pearl stood by the store corner, taking it all in, normal life entering her soul again like a rush of wind.

"I did it!" she said aloud. "I got away. No more 'goyles; no more hustling my ass for money; no more . . ."

A car was filling up at the gas pumps and its driver was staring at her. His look seemed to suggest that he thought she was a hooker.

She looked away from him. *Not any more, man. That was my past life. Now, I'm gonna be a good girl. One who never leaves home for anywhere on the sixth of June!*

The car drove off. She looked at her 666 wristwatch. It had stopped working, but the time here seemed to be evening also. The sun's rays seeped through the wall of trees across the road from the gas station.

Well, I can't remain standing outside here like this, like I am trying to turn tricks. I gotta hitch a ride down to Zanesville, then catch a bus home. But first of all, I gotta make a phone call, see if mom's moved house.

Making a phone call shouldn't prove difficult. Before leaving 666, Pearl had put five hundred dollars into a small purse which she'd afterwards secured in the back pocket of her jeans. She'd also brought along her old Earth credit cards, though she didn't know if those would still be working. But the money would do.

She walked into the convenience store. The young man behind the counter immediately reminded her of Hook; dark and handsome and sporting a goatee. Fleetingly, but with regret, she wondered what the cops would make of things when they found Hook's body by the convenience store wall, four years after he'd gone missing.

She smiled at the clerk, placing Al Gore's book of spells on the counter and leaning on it. "Hi, man. Look, I need to make a phone call to Lancaster. I've lost my cell but I'll pay you to use the store phone."

He looked her over and smiled back. "Store phone's busted, but you can use mine."

"Thanks." She accepted the touchscreen phone from him, then returned it to him. "You're not gonna believe this, man, but I've never used one of these before. Could you please dial for me?"

He looked at her a little strangely then, but nodded. "Yeah, sure. What's the number?"

She gave him her mother's number from memory. The landline, not the cellphone number which she didn't remember.

"It's ringing," he said after a pause, handing the phone back to her. Pearl nodded her gratitude.

"Hello. Harper residence, who's on the line?"

"Hello, mom? Is that you?" But no, the voice hadn't been her mother's. Still though, it sounded eerily familiar.

"Hello?" the woman on the other end of the line said. "Who do you want?"

"Can I speak to Mrs. Harper, please?"

"Yeah, sure. Who should I say is calling?"

"Her daughter Pearl. She'll think it's a joke—I've been missing for—"

"Hey, is this a joke or something?"

"What? A joke? No. Look, I got abducted and . . . just got away . . ."

"Look, I don't know who the hell you are, or what you're trying to accomplish by pretending to be me, but . . ."

Pearl felt like she'd been shot. Now she understood why the voice sounded so familiar. It was her own voice, heard often enough in cellphone recordings back in the old days.

She stood there at the store counter, staring in shock at the clerk.

"Are you alright?" he asked her.

She shook her head in horror. The girl on the phone was speaking again: "Hey, are you still there?"

"Yes, listen. I don't know what's going on here. I assume there's been some mix-up. I'm Pearl Harper, daughter of Melanie Harper, the schoolteacher? Can I just speak to her, please?"

"No, *you* listen, you bitch. *I'm* Pearl Harper. If you don't get off this line right now, I'm going to call the cops and have you arrested for identity theft."

"No, no, no . . . just listen . . ."

But at that moment, she heard the sound of footsteps approaching the girl on the phone, and a voice—clearly her mother's voice—ask: "Pearl, who're you fighting with on the phone?"

And the voice—her own voice—replied: "Dunno, mom, some crazy girl's claiming to be me. Says she was abducted and just got away."

She heard her mother say: "Just hang up, dear, and call the police. They'll be able to trace the call."

"Mom!" Pearl yelled into the phone. "Mom! Hey, you scheming bitch—let me talk to her! Let me talk to her!"

But the other girl—her doppelganger—had already hung up. Pearl was left standing with the dead phone in her hand. She felt limp, blown everywhere by the wind and totally confused.

"Are you sure you're okay?" the store clerk asked with a concerned look on his face. Possibly expecting her to faint, he'd stepped out from behind his counter.

"I don't understand what's happening," Pearl explained miserably. "I got abducted and now there's someone impersonating me at home. And my mother really thinks she's me."

"Damn," the young man said. "But then, that shouldn't be too hard for the cops to clear up. Identity theft's a crime. Just be glad you got away from your abductor. See . . ."

At first she wondered why he'd stopped talking, then realized he was staring down at the floor. Then he looked up and seemed confused.

"Hey, what happened to your feet?" he asked.

Pearl didn't understand what he was talking about until she glanced down at his own feet. Then she began weeping.

Instead of human feet sticking out of the end of his jeans, the young man had large hoofs, like a donkey or a horse would have.

Shocked and with tears in her eyes, she turned and stared at the front entrance, where a well-dressed family of four were just pushing their way into the convenience store. She stared at their feet too. None of them was wearing shoes. All four, male and female alike, had donkey-like hoofs instead of feet.

"Oh shit!" Pearl wept on realizing what had happened. "I made it back to Earth, but it's the wrong Earth!"

Then she fainted.

The End.

ABOUT THE AUTHOR

Wol-vriey is Nigerian, and quite tall.

He believes there actually are things that go bump in the night.

He writes horror fiction—for adults only, please. And also some surrealist stuff.

Wol-vriey blogs at: *http://oddityfarm.wordpress.com*

WOL-VRIEY
BIZARRO AND TRANSGRESSIVE FICTION

BOSTON POSH (BUD MALONE #1)

In 2028 AD, the USA is a nation ravaged by hungry dragons and dinosaurs. In Boston, Massachusetts, private eye Bud Malone is hired to rescue a kidnapped heiress. But nothing is as it seems.

Malone works to unravel a tangled web involving Boston Chinatown, a 200-year-old woman with a 9-year-old body, white robots, a human-liver-eating psychopath, a golem, a porcelain dragon, and a snake goddess with a crush on him. There's also a woman obsessed with chicken sex. Then Malone meets Posh Lane, a gorgeous call girl who's desperate to quit her pimp.

Romantic sparks ignite between Posh and Malone, but Posh's past suddenly catches up with her in a BIG way. To save Posh, Malone agrees to run a quest for Earth's new rulers, the Forks. But, Malone has no idea that agreeing to the Fork's odd request will send him on the weirdest trip he's ever been on in his life.

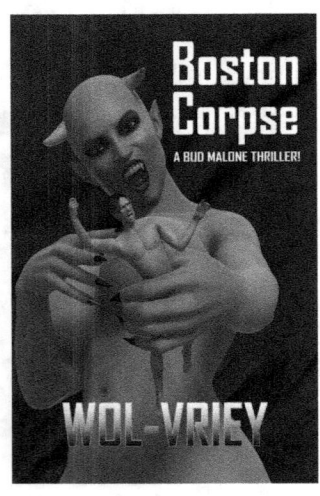

BOSTON CORPSE (BUD MALONE #2)

MAGIC CAN BE MURDER! - Drag queen Lucy Tang is back in Boston, and is hell-bent on settling her vindetta against casino owner Sookie Ling. And suddenly, Bud Malone, PI, has the case of his life to resolve.

When Boston's robot police force are baffled by a mind transfer case, they come to Malone for help. The one person who can likely help Malone out here is the witch Soledad Bathory. But Soledad seems to know a lot more than she's telling him. It's a case not made easier when Malone meets Soledad's beautiful cousin, Josephine 'Slave' Bailey. Slave has her own plans for Malone, most of which involve teaching him BDSM and making him her new Master.

Oh, and Rick Rogers owes Sookie Ling a whole lot of money, a gambling debt that's going to be literally Hell to pay!

BOSTON CORPSE - Not your average detective novel!

Burning Bulb
PUBLISHING

WOL-VRIEY
BIZARRO AND TRANSGRESSIVE FICTION

BOSTON LUST (BUD MALONE #3)

"Bless it, Father, for she has sinned."

Seven murdered gay women, all their bodies completely drained of blood. All also with large parts of their bodies dissolved away like acid has been pumped into their veins.

Bud Malone has to find the female vampire preying on Boston's lesbian population.

Then Malone meets the beautiful Trudi Carmen and the case gets even more tangled. Trudi needs Malone's help in recovering a ring that's gone missing. But how in the world is one little black ring related to either the dead women or their killer?

Resolving this case will lead Malone deep into Lucy Tang's legacy—The Abstracta. And then to the city of Genesis.

Boston Lust—Just when you thought Bean Town was safe to visit again.

HELL DANCER

Six people find themselves trapped in Detention, a nightmare realm where the demonic Schoolmaster is hell-bent on reforming them . . . until they die.

Porn superstar Venus Deluxe came to Springfield, MA to party, and next found her life hanging by a thread. One wrong answer will mean her death.

Suspended BPD detective Tanya Rockford was trying to stop one kind of violence, but found a terrifying another. With her and her companion's lives hanging in the balance, it's going to take all of her courage and resourcefulness to escape this hell she's stumbled into.

Porn stud Chad Cannon has made a career from his ten-inch penis. Here in Detention, however, it's his brains that matter. He'll soon be hoping all the pot he's smoked over the years hasn't completely messed up his memory.

The three students, Sherri, Jordan, and Mike? They were all just in the wrong place at the right time. Will anyone survive Detention? The evil Schoolmaster doesn't plan on letting that happen . . .

Burning Bulb
PUBLISHING

WOL-VRIEY
BIZARRO AND TRANSGRESSIVE FICTION

VAGINA MUNDI

Rachel Risk is a professional thief with super-strong hair that can stretch like tentacles to manipulate objects. Ashley Status has both a digitally augmented brain, and 'muscle-purses' in her arms and legs in which she stores inflatable objects—cars, guns, rocket launchers, etc.

When Raye is framed as the fall girl in a jewel robbery, the pair flee Chicago's vengeful robot gangsters and take refuge in the Hotel Bizarre, where the gorgeous 'vagina singer,' Femina, is performing for a week.

But the Hotel Bizarre is even stranger than its name suggests, and very soon Raye and Ash are involved in an deadly adventure, a struggle for survival the likes of which they'd never imagined possible—with loads of deviant sex, drugs, music, and violence at every turn. And just what is the old woman in the skin desert really doing with all those cats glued to her walls?

VAGINA MUNDI—a Bizarro Hymn in praise of WOMAN!

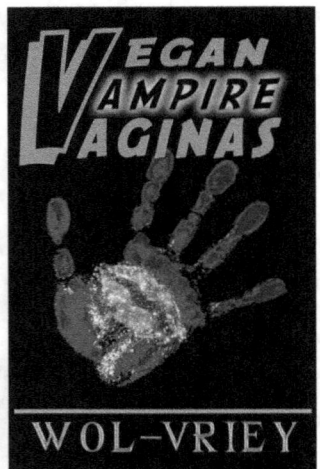

VEGAN VAMPIRE VAGINAS

The biggest bank heist in US history. And Tom Palmer can't remember pulling it off. And no, this isn't your standard case of amnesia. After a one-night-stand gone horribly wrong, Boston salesman Tom Palmer wakes up with a vagina implanted in his left hand. Then his day gets worse.

Tom is transported across space-time to a nightmare version of Boston, one where the Bizarro virus has transformed half the population into cannibals. Worst of all, Tom discovers that in this new Boston, he's the infamous gangster Pussypalm, wanted for robbing the Federal Reserve Bank of Boston a year ago. He also learns that the vagina in his hand is prophetic, i.e. it talks . . . after sex.

With 130 people left dead during his bank heist and six billion dollars missing, Tom knows he's living on borrowed time. It is in his best interests not to remember anything. Because once he does . . .

Burning Bulb
PUBLISHING

WOL-VRIEY
BIZARRO AND TRANSGRESSIVE FICTION

VEGAN ZOMBIE APOCALYPSE

In the post-apocalypse worlderness, zombies rule the earth. They're allergic to meat, and brains literally make them explode. Zombies now eat blood potatoes, parasitic tubers grown in the flesh of humancows corralled in maximum security farms. Two fugitives meet in the ancient ruins of Texas. The first is Soil 15-f, a womancow who's escaped her farm a week before she's due to be killed and her blood potato crop harvested. The second fugitive is Able Kane, former head necros food technician, now sentenced to death for heresy. But Soil is no ordinary humancow.

Unknown to herself, she's the vegan zombie agricultural revolution, and the zombies desperately want her back. And the necros equally desperately want Able Kane dead. He's fled with a forbidden discovery which will reshape the world for the worse if used. And Able is just hardheaded/misguided enough to use it.

MELANIE NEMESIS CATCHPOLE

In Springfield, Massachusetts, Melanie Catchpole is hired to fetch back a magic teddy bear worth millions of dollars from a warehouse across town. Problem is, the warehouse is down in Springfield's O-Zone—that totally weird sector of the city where Bizarro fell to Earth. The 'O' is a fairytale land, a place where dreams and nightmares literally live and breathe..

Worse still, the gingers—mutant cannibals—prowl the O. The gingers have already eaten everyone else Melanie's employers sent to get back the magic teddy bear.

Accompanied by the handsome but ruthless Doug Fisher (who she finds sexy but doesn't dare entrust her heart to), Melanie enters the O-Zone. Melanie and Doug are instantly caught up in an adventure they'd never have believed credible even if written as fiction . . . and Melanie's used to experiencing the very weird as the norm.

And now, additionally, there's a mystery to unravel: What does the dark, freezing-cold being called The Fixer want with Mary, the barkeep's daughter?

Burning Bulb
PUBLISHING

WOL-VRIEY
BIZARRO AND TRANSGRESSIVE FICTION

BIG TROUBLE IN LITTLE ASS

From Bizarro master storyteller Wol-vriey comes a truly weird western tale that will leave you awe-struck and on the edge of your seat...

In the town named Little Ass, tight-assed prostitute Rosa overhears a gunslinger's plans to assassinate rancher Edison Bennett. Once the badass Bennett learns of the plot, he ensures there'll be hell to pay for any attempt on his life!

Yes, it's going to take all of gunslinger Jude's shooting prowess, his eclectic collection of strange firearms, a trusty horse that requires an owners' manual, and the help of the lovely and invigorating Nell (who's EXTREMELY odd when the going gets weird), to survive the Bizarro hell that Edison Bennett unleashes in order to hold onto the land that he'd stolen from Madam Zizi.

BIZARRO 101 (A BASIC PRIMER)

Welcome to the strange place:

A collection of 37 flash fiction stories designed to introduce one to the Bizarro/New Weird Genre.

Weird, dreamy, nightmarish, absurd, sad, surreal, humorous . . . this collection of tales is all this and more.

***

"This primer is the very essence of any and all styles and types of Bizarro writing. Wol-vriey collects, distills, and bottles up these 37 tiny stories for your sensory enjoyment. This is an absolute must-read for anyone new to the genre, because it demonstrates the scope of what Bizarro is, and what it can be."
—Teresa Pollack, Bizarro commentator and blogger

Burning Bulb
PUBLISHING

WOL-VRIEY
BIZARRO AND TRANSGRESSIVE FICTION

Dr. Orgasm

Courtney Taylor is young, intelligent, beautiful, and successful. She also has a boyfriend who loves her deeply. The problem is, no matter what Courtney does, she can't climax during sex.

When Florence Rigid's communist forces destroy the city of Metaphor, Courtney and her friends Teresa, Highball, Miki, and Heather are cast into the midst of a quest to find the only person able to save the land of Innuendo—Dr. Carol Orgasm, wanted by the communists for developing the O-Pill, a wonder drug that grants women sexual ecstasy on demand.

The communists will do anything to get their hands on the O-Pill and prevent its reaching the millions of Innuendo's women. But Courtney desperately wants that pill too. And so it's now a race between Courtney and the communists to find Dr. Orgasm first.

And Courtney has no choice but to win this race. She must win it: For her own orgasm . . . and for the freedom of female sexuality everywhere.

PUSSY TRANSMISSION

Pussy Transmission were the most decadent Pop Art ensemble of the 90's. Led by the beautiful painter Isis Lynch, the trio revolutionized the art world. Then suddenly, without explanation, Pussy Transmission vanished into historical obscurity. Now, twenty years later, three women come to Lynch Place. Lily and Nina are journalists desperate to interview Isis Lynch. Raven, on the other hand, wants to find her boyfriend, who's gone missing inside Isis's house. Raven's worried—she's heard that Pussy Transmission broke up because Isis began dabbling in black magic . . . with devastating results. All three women will shortly wish they'd never left home. Particularly once the rats in Lynch Place start warning them that they're going to die . . . and Raven meets Betty Butcher, the bouncy supernatural psycho who's intent on chopping her into bits. Pussy Transmission, Baby! Just because . . .

Burning Bulb
PUBLISHING

WOL-VRIEY
BIZARRO AND TRANSGRESSIVE FICTION

GIRLS ARE NOT SMILING
Welcome To The Road Trip From Hell

Pagan is demon-possessed.

Lori is suicidal.

Britt is just terminally pissed off.

Meet three young Boston women on the run from the law, each with problems that will fuse into more than the sum of their individual parts, becoming a holocaust of sex and violence and terror, a literal rain of blood and horror and gore and evil.

And if that wasn't already bad enough, Pagan's pet demon is slowly transforming her into something both unspeakable and unholy. Truly, these girls aren't smiling.

BLUE NIGHTMARES
Consummate EVIL is coming. It is relentless and unavoidable. It is Blue.

Jessica Schreiber is seeing things. Very horrible things. Since arriving in Raynham for what should have been a relaxing vacation, she's been seeing *The Big Blue*.

Jessica is smelling things too—dead and rotting things that she can't see. She is sure those dead and rotting things are dead people. Lots of dead people.

Jessica's worst nightmares will soon become her reality. Her reality will soon become a terrifying nightmare.

The tentacled residents of the House of Death have a lot that they wish to show Jessica Schreiber. They have a lot that they wish to tell her. But will she survive long enough to learn their lessons?

Burning Bulb
PUBLISHING

WOL-VRIEY
BIZARRO AND TRANSGRESSIVE FICTION

BRAINCHEW

It was supposed to be a simple jewel heist, but it went badly wrong. Chuck got shot and died.

Lance hid his friend's corpse in the Pleasant Street Cemetery. But that was a big mistake—there was something undead, something extremely hungry . . . something eXXXtremely horrible, buried in the Pleasant Street Cemetery.

And Lance had just woken it up.

They called the monster Brainchew because it ate brains. Human brains. And it preferred those brains fresh from the heads . . . of the living.

And now it was awake again, Brainchew planned on feeding big-time tonight. Oh hell yes, it did.

BRAINCHEW 2: OUT OF THEIR HEADS

After Tiff Hooper recognizes Josh Penham, the man who abducted her and kept her in his basement and abused her, she brings her three friends to Raynham for a night of well-deserved revenge on him.

Only things don't go according to plan.

It is never a good idea to leave a corpse in Raynham's Pleasant Street Cemetery. You run the very real risk of awakening what lies underground there. And that thing—Brainchew—is more horrible and more evil than anything the average mind conceives of even in its worst nightmares.

Brainchew is back! And this time the monster is extra-hungry. But there are plenty of delicious human brains about tonight, and Brainchew intends to eat them all before dawn.

Burning Bulb
PUBLISHING

WOL-VRIEY
BIZARRO AND TRANSGRESSIVE FICTION

DARIA: AN EROTIC NIGHTMARE

Even the best laid women can go wrong.

Daria Simpson is HUNGRY. She's HUNGRY for sex and bloodshed and death.

Shelly Parker just wanted to have a threesome with her boyfriend Craig and her best friend Erica. Everything was shaping up nicely for their weekend of sexual fun and games, until they stopped at the creepy Crossway Diner and met Daria.

From the moment they met Daria, EVERYTHING went wrong for them; and it went wrong in the most horrific and terrifying of ways!

Daria: Paranormal service has been resumed.

WET BONES

Greg is about learning the hard way that you don't mess with Aunt Grace.

Nine completely fleshless skeletons recovered in the Massachusetts woods. Two detectives on the trail of a horrible, hungry monster.

Broken-hearted Allie Jackson has a date with a creature from Hell.

Things are about to get well out of hand for everyone, and in horrifying, terrifying ways they don't expect.

Burning Bulb
PUBLISHING

WOL-VRIEY
BIZARRO AND TRANSGRESSIVE FICTION

MR. UGLY

When a rotting corpse appears and starts butchering Raynham's youths, there's really only one question that needs answering:

Is this faceless and rotting monster Peter Howard, or isn't it?

Problem is, Peter Howard died 15 years ago. So how can he possibly be back from the dead and murdering people with such relentless and incredible brutality?

Peter's mother Malicia, who's just been released from the lunatic asylum may have the answers to the crazy puzzle, but the two detectives investigating the deaths don't even know the right questions to ask her yet.

BRUTAL

Jane Winters is 28 years old.

She works as a checkout cashier in a department store. She's an attractive woman with a winning personality. She has both a photographic memory and an I.Q. of 189.

She's met the man of her dreams.

But she's also a cannibal with a unique and very scary mode of operation.

The group known as TULIP (The Urban Legend Investigation People) are out to either prove or disprove the legend of Insane Jane.

But have TULIP bitten off more than they can chew?

Burning Bulb
PUBLISHING

WOL-VRIEY
BIZARRO AND TRANSGRESSIVE FICTION

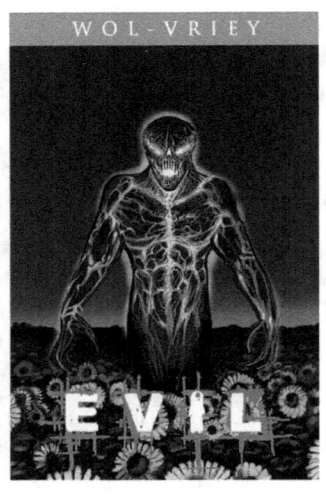

EVIL

The Evil began the week before Sylvia Stewart's 30th birthday.

Cathy Higgins died.

The Bargainer resurrected Cathy . . . for a price.

The price? Cathy's father Ronan had to plant some seeds for him.

But these were no ordinary seeds the Bargainer gave to Ronan Higgins. These were seeds from Hell: seeds which required human flesh as both soil and fertilizer.

And meanwhile, the unsuspecting Sylvia Stewart went ahead with the plans for her birthday party, which was to be held on Ronan Higgins' sunflower farm . . .

666

Ohio's State Route 666 stretches 14.7 miles between Zanesville and Dresden.

Most days, it's just a normal road with a funny name.

But for six minutes on the 6th of June each year, Route 666 becomes a gateway to somewhere else . . . a gateway to Hell.

Each year 13 unfortunates get trapped in the 666 underworld, with no way to get back home.

This year though, things are going to be very different. For one thing, there are currently a whole lot of turbulent human emotions at play in the underworld. And also . . . the psycho Al Gore is just about completing his collection of human heads.

And . . . what the hell is a church doing in Hell, of all places?

Burning Bulb
PUBLISHING